EMPIRES FOR THE MAKING

"Well," I said, "we now know how to become emperors. Pick our planet, and we can take it over. We could even have one each . . . or maybe a little galactic empire."

"Let's you and me invade Earth," suggested Karen. "I have this plan, see, for setting the world to rights . . ."

"Not Earth," I said, shaking my head. "Why not?"

"Problems of supply," I said. "Also problems of demand. Earth is suffering from a surfeit of puppet-strings already. It has to be a colony—a virgin colony. We'd have to be there at the very beginning . . . just like James Wildeblood."

"Wildeblood and Machiavelli and Alexander the Great," muttered Karen.

"Precisely," I said.

WILDEBLOOD'S EMPIRE

Brian M. Stableford

DAW BOOKS, INC.
DONALD A. WOLLHEIM, PUBLISHER

1301 Avenue of the Americas
New York, N. Y.   10019

FIRST PRINTING, OCTOBER 1977

1 2 3 4 5 6 7 8 9

PRINTED IN U.S.A.

1

I left the house by a small door at the back that had been left on the latch. I guess it was what they'd call the "tradesmen's entrance." I was glad to find it—climbing out of windows is so undignified. It let me out into a part of the grounds that were tastefully hidden from the front drive—the kitchen gardens, stocked and laid out for function rather than for show. I set off between the cabbages and the runner beans, heading north until I could veer east without wreaking havoc among the plants.

I put a hundred yards or so between myself and the house before I switched on the flashlight to help me on my way. There were several second and third story windows which still showed cracks of light through their drawn curtains. Going early to bed wasn't a universal habit hereabouts. . . . In fact, no sooner had the last of the masters retired than the first of the servants would be getting up. I was pretty confident that no one was following me, but it seemed like a sensible precaution not to show a light until it became necessary. When I finally did use the flash it was because I'd run into a thicket and was both masked from the house and well and truly stuck. The bushes here had never invented thorns but some species had helical filamentous shoots that tangled ankles beautifully.

I used a small knife to cut myself free, wishing it were a machete.

I didn't have far to go. In daylight, it would have taken me about fifteen minutes, but it wasn't daylight and I wasn't going the easy way around. I stayed in the star-shadow of the trees wherever possible, and switched off the light when I had to cross open ground. There was a stiff breeze blowing in off the sea, and it struck shivers into me whenever I was exposed to it, but the trees afforded me shelter from it most of the way. It was late spring, and it should have been warmer, but the weather wasn't trying this season. The breeding cycle had started late and the corn in the fields was slow in maturing. It didn't seem as if it was going to be much of a summer for Wildeblood's empire. Or for us.

I climbed the iron railings that bounded the grounds of the house, thinking for the fortieth time what a criminal waste of iron it must have been in the days when it was built. The colonists had plenty now for their immediate necessities, but in the first hard decades you don't expect a seven-mile stretch of six-foot railings to come high on the priority list. But James Wildeblood, by all accounts, had been a man of somewhat eccentric priorities. I walked beside the road, in the shadow of the railings, for a little way, prepared to dive into the creeping weeds which decked them at the first sign of company. But I crossed the road into the woods when the time came without having seen a suspicious shadow or heard the ghost of a hoofbeat.

The stars shone steadily, looking for all the world like Earthly stars. Even in the dark, colony worlds aren't often indistinguishable from home, but this one was as good a match to rural north Europe as we were likely to find. No doubt its deserts were a dead spit for the Sahara as well. The thing that really encouraged the illusion that I might be back home was the Milky Way. The patterns of the bright stars against the backcloth of the void were meaningless, but that long river of stardust looked the same as it ever does. Somehow, with a streak of parochial romanticism, I thought of it as *belonging* to Earth's skies, and shining here only as a symbol of kinship between the human worlds. The locals, no doubt, thought that it was Wildeblood's galaxy . . . maybe Wildeblood's universe.

The world had officially gone into the records back home as Poseidon. (Official naming policy is horribly unimaginative—watery worlds get watery names, and Oceania and Thalassa had both been taken.) But James Wildeblood had considered that there was only one possible name for use in the colony. It promoted identification between the physical world and the social environment, enhanced the development of the concept of an all-embracing natural order. Here, *all* was Wildeblood. If they'd had to find a new name for God . . .

There was a group of cottages ahead of me, and I knew that I'd looped back to the road at the correct spot. They were all dark, all silent. For effect, there should have been a gravedigger about his lonely work. I'd always wanted to say "Alas, poor Yorick!" But the gravediggers worked by day . . . and the stonemasons.

There were no iron railings round the cemetery. Its boundary was marked by a chain of wooden stakes with long, thin laths of wood connecting them. It was a symbolic boundary. Also a flexible one. The graveyard had room for growth—room, in fact, for virtually limitless expansion. James Wildeblood had believed in graves. Proper graves. Marked graves. Graves to remember people by. He had been very strong on tradition—had made every attempt to start a lot of them. One day, maybe, when his children's children had conquered the world, this island (where it had all started) would have nothing except the house (*the* house) and graves. A legion of the dead, equipped with massive

7

stones as identity tabs and testimonials. An awesome array. By then, interogression should have carried Wildeblood genes into every last stagnant eddy of the gene pool, and everyone would claim descent from the Great Ancestor. They would make pilgrimages here from every corner of the world, to find the story of their history written in the stones.

It's easier to store records on a computer, and if you're desperate you can always use pencil and paper. But they don't quite have the personality of a forest of stone slabs rooted amid the rotting bones.

Some of the markers were only a foot or two high, others four or five. But it was in the height that they varied—in terms of basal area they were virtually identical. The plots of ground they labelled were identical, too, and not over-generous. Three feet by two was considered enough. I didn't know whether they buried people slanted or folded or tied in a knot. I hadn't asked. I didn't really want to know.

Even the taller stones were unadorned. No crosses. No angels. No grotesques. It couldn't be much fun being a stonemason. Their artistic talents were more-or-less limited to the style of the lettering which cut the epitaphs into the stone.

I played the light around, wondering if all the tall stones marked aristocratic graves and so on down the social scale. But the small sample I looked at didn't bear that out. And there were too many tall ones anyhow. I suspected that the variation was probably random, to break up the deadly evenness of the pattern. The dead, I guessed, would all be equal—a reminder and a promise to set against the gross inequality of the living.

Even such details, I thought, Wildeblood planned. He must have been one hell of a character. Here, written in the whole history of the colony, written literally in the stones, was the legacy of an obsession, of one of the most curious cases of paranoid creativity ever known.

All the stones had names, dates, marriages, children. And comments. Brief, concise, often rather strange. The names I looked at and over. I didn't take them in. There were too many, all kinds. The dates, too, I didn't pay much attention to, except to note that longevity wasn't usual. It was rare for anyone to live much beyond fifty. That wasn't for lack of medical knowledge—or even in more recent times—for lack of resources. It was because colony life was, and had been, tough. Even so, fifty was low, and I wondered whether it had been tougher than we suspected. But the part of the cemetery I was passing through had been dug between 80 and 90, local figuring (after the landing, of course) and it represented the fate of one of the earliest generations. Not a representative sample.

The one thing which did make an impression on me was the epitaphs. They weren't long and they weren't eulogistic. They certainly weren't versified or sentimentalized, and they lacked the classic touch of irony you often find on old Christian graves on Earth. The epitaphs said things like: *She was strong; He was a craftsman; He fished the sea.* Statements of occupation, or of *contribution*. They delineated roles within the colony. There were some ambiguous or ambitious ones: *He helped shape the future; He was a pioneer; He was a leader.* There seemed to be no determined attempt to avoid repetition. The commonest inscription by far, and perhaps the most telling, was the simple statement: *She bore children.* Just that. It didn't even have to say how many, because their names were recorded beneath the name and dates of the woman herself.

Added together, though—taking the display of

stones as a whole—the inscriptions didn't give the impression of mere functionality or matter-of-factness. They gave the impression of community self-congratulation, of pride—as if these things were all that *needed* to be said, as if they were *enough*. A collective false modesty.

I moved slowly through the stone forest, swinging the light back and forth. Even after I knew the pattern and sensed something of the idea embodied in it, I looked for something like a mausoleum—something extra special. I didn't find it.

When I heard something moving to my left I spun on my heel, feeling a sudden surge of adrenalin thrusting up within me like an internal fist. I hadn't realized how keyed-up I'd become. All my fears had lain subconsciously, but nevertheless active. Walking in a cemetery can't help but stir the deep-seated anxieties within us. They are not, in themselves, fear of ghosts or ghouls—these are merely the ideas that an imagination may attach to them to make them comprehensible. They are more basic, perhaps to do with our innate psychological relationship with death.

In any case, when the light picked out his white face a lance of fear, a genuine shudder, passed through me.

It wasn't a very pretty face, but in daylight it would have seemed merely ugly, not disturbing at all. The eyes were deep-set, the mouth thick-lipped. The nose was large—not bulbous, but pointed, seeming to project unnaturally far from its root in the turbinal bones.

He was tall—somewhat taller than I, and powerfully built. He didn't look like a musician, although that had been his ostensible role when I'd seen him earlier in the day, in the town.

A wandering minstrel? He certainly qualified on the grounds of thread and patches ... his clothes were worn and untidy. He probably did a lot of travelling. He was a musician, but also a carrier of information—news, rumor, person-to-person messages. In all probability he would be a mender, too, a man of considerable general practical knowledge. And a thief. But his role would be a necessary one in a widely-dispersed colony like this one, where there was no efficient communicative network—and might never be if James Wildeblood's priorities continued to be served. His role, too, would be the perfect one to cloak a rebel—if not the leader of the underground, then its life-blood. Not just a thief, but a king of thieves . . . the other hegemony . . . the anti-aristocracy.

"Your name's Alexander?" He said. His voice was sharp, pitched higher than one might expect of such a big man. But I'd heard him sing high *and* low earlier in the day.

"Who were you expecting?" I said dryly. "The Scarlet Pimpernel?" I let the sarcasm smother my untimely nervousness.

He didn't laugh. He didn't even get the joke.

"The appointed place," he said, "is this way."

He turned away. I followed. I didn't see that it mattered much. We'd found one another. But he, apparently, was a stickler for the script. In the true melodramatic tradition he'd invited me to meet him at James Wildeblood's grave, and nearby obviously wasn't good enough. He took me into the oldest part of the cemetery, where the grass between the graves grew a little higher, and the weeds upon them a little wilder.

The most important gravestone of them all wasn't particularly massive. There was no mausoleum, no vault. There wasn't even anything special in the inscription. The covert assumption was that people didn't need reminding who and what this man had been. No birthdate was given—Earth dates didn't count here. The date of his death was 33. I could deduce from that that he'd been seventy-odd when he finally dropped dead, but from the point of view of his descendants only the years he'd spent on *this* world were to be remembered.

"He took the place that became available in the natural course of events," said the big man. "Between a shoemaker and a fisherman. He expected to be admired for that. The humility of the omnipotent."

"He could afford it," I said.

"But someday," said the other, "he'll be forgotten. And then there'll be nothing here to sort him out from all the rest. In time, he can be made to vanish."

I doubted it. I doubted it very much. He'd contributed too much just to the *naming* of everything here. The "James" might decay and die from memory in a thousand years, but not the "Wildeblood." I doubted whether it could ever lose its meaning entirely. But I hadn't come to argue.

"Who are you?" I asked.

"I don't use my name," he said. "Names help people to remember. I let people remember me by what I am, what I do. That way I can be confused with a dozen other men."

I thought it undiplomatic to point out to him that the other dozen were unlikely to have such remarkable and memorable features. Cyrano de Bergerac, as I remembered it, had been quick to take offense if anyone suggested that his nose was anything out of the ordinary. There was no point in taking chances.

"Okay," I said. "You're nameless. What do you want?"

"To speak to you."

"I guessed that much," I replied, with some impatience. "You'd hardly make an appointment to

12

meet me in a graveyard at dead of night unless you had something to say—something which couldn't be said while Elkanah's flapping ears were working nineteen to the dozen. I'm cold. I don't want to play games. Say what you have to say."

"I have to be careful," he told me.

And that was fair enough. He had indeed. He'd already exposed himself. He had no way of knowing how we stood relative to Philip Wildeblood and his *ancien régime*. He didn't want me turning him in, and he didn't want to give away more than was strictly necessary in case I did—or in case our meeting was subsequently to become known. He had a vested interest in playing the mystery man, and in his place I wouldn't have trusted me as far as I could throw a gravestone, either. He was putting himself at some risk. James Wildeblood's code of laws didn't have any death penalties, but it embodied some very strenuous ways of working off debts to society. Not pleasant ones, either.

"We thought that it was about time we made contact," he said. "I came down from Skerry some days ago. I've asked questions in the town. You landed thirty days ago?"

"Thirty-two," I corrected him.

"And you've been . . . inspecting the colony."

"You could put it that way. We came to help—to find out what problems the colony has faced in adapting to Poseidon and to help solve any that looked dangerous. We've been looking at the crops in the field, the health of the people—all areas of endeavor. Philip has co-operated fully . . . even to the extent of providing very efficient guides."

The last comment was ironic. Our guides were also our keepers. They were with us at all times. We were followed everywhere. Philip was co-operating all right, but he was also watching our every move like a hawk. In all probability, if we hadn't been such good, innocent outworlders this last month the vigilance might not have relaxed sufficiently for me to slip away that night.

The big man didn't understand my reference to "Poseidon", but he didn't query it.

"You want to help," he said.

"That's right," I affirmed.

"And the people? You find them healthy?"

I had to answer that one cautiously. "Their physical condition isn't quite what we'd find on Earth," I said. "There are certain physiological anomalies, but they're consistent within the population. We expect to find slight changes, adaptations to new conditions. Often we don't understand just how and why the balance changes, but it always does. All in all, though, there seems to be no significant deficiency or maladjustment in the population."

"Suppose I told you that the people are not healthy?" he said.

I shrugged. I didn't know what he was getting at. Was there a considerable sector of the population that was being hidden from us? It seemed unlikely.

"Show me evidence," I said.

"And if there *were* evidence?" he countered, "What then?"

"That depends," I said. "On what kind of evidence. And of what." We weren't getting anywhere playing cat-and-mouse like that, but he wasn't in an hurry to give out with what he had and I wasn't going to commit myself in any way no matter what. The haggling couldn't be cut short, under those circumstances.

"Our future here depends on the outcome of your visit," he said. "Isn't that so?"

"Could be," I said, with truth enough. He was jumping to wrong conclusions, but I let him. Never let the other man underestimate you. Always encourage him to credit you with more than you've got. It oils the wheels of negotiation. Nathan had taught me that.

"You scare Philip," he went on. "He thinks you may be a threat to his power. Are you?"

That was a more specific question, and a deadlier one.

"I don't know," I said. I didn't go on. Anything I added would only lead into deep water.

"We're prepared to help you," said the tall man, coming to the point at his own chosen speed. "We're prepared to show you things that Philip wouldn't permit you to see. But in return, we want your help."

"I can't promise anything," I said. "If you think the information you're offering will change our attitude to Philip then it may be in your interests to let us have it. But we aren't here to start or support a rebellion. We can only act within our own brief. But if Philip is concealing something which is a threat to the health and prospects of this colony, then we ought to know."

I knew that I wasn't offering him much. I was encouraging him all I could, but I didn't really have a lot to bargain with. On the other hand, he'd already taken the risk. He'd passed me the message arranging the meeting. If he didn't give me anything it was his loss, his wasted efforts.

"You've only scratched the surface so far," he said. "You don't know what's underneath Wildeblood's rule."

I stayed silent. Maybe I didn't. Very probably, in fact.

"You have to help us," he said. "When you know, you'll see that you have to help us."

I still didn't answer. There *was* no answer.

"I'm going to give you two things," he said. "I'm

taking a big risk. But it's important—to you as well as to us. I'm not going to say too much. If they find what I've given you it's nothing to do with me. I deny everything. They'll believe you if you turn them over now and have me arrested—but once you've started to look into them on your own account, to find out what they are, you're guilty too. I advise you not to tell them."

After that long and rather unimpressive speech he reached into his coat and brought out a small package about the size of a folded finger. He passed it over to me while he transferred something else to his other hand.

"It's not much," he said. "The stuff's precious. Analyze it. Find out what it is, what it does, where it comes from. And find out what you can do with it."

"That's rather a lot of things to find out," I commented.

"Can you do it?" He seemed anxious.

"I can try," I conceded. Privately, I was fairly confident. The lab had the facilities to do just about anything in that line.

Then he passed me the other item—a piece of paper. It was a domestic product, thick and handmade.

"There are numbers on it," he said, and I made to open it for inspection. "Don't look now. The numbers are a code. I don't have the key. If you can crack it, you may find the contents interesting. If you do, then it may be possible to trade. We need the key—and we have the rest of the message. I don't know whether you can crack it or not ... but try. It's important—to us, and maybe to you as well."

I hesitated. I didn't like the idea of coded messages. It seemed a bit stupid—so close to melodrama it had to be a joke. But he was serious. And this was Wildeblood, and something more like the Middle Ages than the twenty-fourth century.

"Can't you tell me any more?" I asked.

"No," he replied. He was lying. He was holding something in reserve. It made sense, from his end. He had to keep something. Maybe he'd already given us too much.

"I take it you've tried to crack the code yourself?" I said.

"For a long time," he said. "For a very long time. But what do we know about codes?"

What do we? I asked myself. Somehow, the UN hadn't felt it necessary to attach a cryptographer to the crew. But Nathan had a devious mind. Maybe he could do it.

"How do I contact you?" I asked.

"You don't," he said. "Don't ever try. It's too dangerous. If you started asking questions.... They're too careful. I'll get to you again. Soon. Don't waste any time."

"I won't," I assured him. "But don't expect miracles. No miracles of *any* kind."

He knew what I meant. It didn't make him happy, but he was a realist. A hopeful one maybe, but a realist. He'd had to take the chance of approaching us, just in case there was an opportunity for him, but he wasn't expecting any messiahs, or armies of liberation either.

It was all a rather sorry mess: meetings in graveyards, cautious interchanges of semi-promises. But under the circumstances . . .

I couldn't help thinking of it as crude melodrama, but to him it was normal. A way of life . . .

We parted. He disappeared into the gloom, carrying no light. I made my way carefully through the maze of stones the way I'd come. It was going to be a hard day tomorrow—not the sort of day I'd

17

have preferred to face without a good night's sleep. But needs must when the devil drives.

And I had the feeling that on Wildeblood/Poseidon there was a devil, somewhere, doing some hard driving.

2

Next day, when I went back to the *Daedalus* after breakfast, I was, of course, followed. It wasn't Elkanah, my appointed guide—he was a servant, but one of some status, above such menial tasks as the daily spying detail. It was, in fact, a younger man with blond hair. He would have been easy to spot in a crowd, and he didn't take any trouble to conceal either himself or his purpose.

I didn't like that. I didn't care for being watched so closely, but even more I didn't care for the carelessly blatant way it was done. It became a kind of insult—almost an intimidation. I had complained once, but the way the complaint was received had simply supplemented the insult. Zarnecki—Philip's right-hand man and the one who seemed to hand out all the orders—had simply said that it was for our protection. When I'd expressed a desire to be responsible for my own protection he'd said—very smoothly—that we were on his world and that he and Philip *were* responsible, and that there was no way he could square it with his own conscience to let us roam around unprotected. He hadn't used precisely those words, but that had been the gist of his meaning.

I didn't like Zarnecki. I didn't like any of them, but Zarnecki least of all. He was tall and slim, olive-skinned and black-haired but with strangely colored eyes—deep blue around the pupil's rim shading to grey-brown at the iris's extremity. He gave the impression of being extremely fond of himself while not thinking too highly of others—any others.

He was, of course, fairly closely related to Philip. Just about every member of the upper crust—whether they lived in the house or elsewhere—was a cousin a couple of times removed. I got the impression the aristocracy had been formed entirely by the marrying of the early Wildeblood children. James had had four—two of each.

I generally thought of Zarnecki as the opposition, although I wasn't really sure we had grounds for conflict with Philip's coterie—not, at any rate, grounds which Nathan and standing orders would recognize. Zarnecki was the front man—the executive arm of the dictatorial clique. It was him who set the men to watch us and report our every move, even though he acted in Philip's name and, undoubtedly, with Philip's full approval.

It was, therefore, Zarnecki I cursed as the blond youth ambled along the dirt road in my wake. In the early days I had occasionally stopped and let my shadow catch up, hoping that the irony of the gesture might discourage them. But it didn't. The closer they got, the better they seemed to like it. So now I let them keep the full distance of their ungenerous discretion.

Pete Rolving and Karen Karelia were aboard the *Daedalus*, having been appointed to look after the baby for the duration. Nathan and I were staying at the house—guests of the State—and other members of the expedition—Mariel, Conrad and Linda —had gone to the mainland on a special project. Unlike Florida and Dendra, where we'd previously called, Poseidon had intelligent indigenes. Mariel had gone out to exercise her special talents and make contact.

Pete and Karen were both up and about when I got there—he overstaying the end of one shift and she up early for another. They kept the routine religiously, with what seemed to me to be ridiculous untiring devotion to the letter of their duty. Karen, I knew, would have been grateful for a chance to get out and into whatever action there might be, but with the personnel shortage there was little chance. Pete didn't mind. He got separation anxiety if he stepped outside the airlock.

Pete made me a cup of coffee. It was one thing that the colonists didn't have and didn't have any reasonable substitute for.

"I contacted the bad guys last night," I told them. "Or the good guys, depending on whether or not you're a Robin Hood fan."

"How?" asked Pete.

"Slipped out after dark. Met him in the cemetery in response to his hoarsely whispered invitation. Cloak-and-dagger all the way. He's a dead ringer for Cyrano de Bergerac, but he also plays guitar."

"And you signed an agreement in blood, no doubt?" contributed Karen.

"Not exactly," I replied. "I wasn't in my best conspiratorial mood. Couldn't really enter into the spirit of the thing. But he tried hard. Gave me a message in code."

They didn't know whether to believe me. I took out the piece of paper and showed them. I also had the package and I dropped that on the table too.

"What's that?" asked Pete.

"I don't know yet."

Karen studied the numbers on the piece of paper. Pete peered over her shoulder.

They went: 688668 . 585775 . 971875 . 7 . 74 . 679234 . 1145874 . 16831 . 598589966.

"Not exactly a long message, is it?" she said.

"That's just a sample," I told her. "He says we might get the rest if we crack it."

"And how are we supposed to crack it without

the rest?" asked Pete. "How the hell can we do a frequency analysis with only nine words—if they *are* words? Could be a string of telephone numbers for all we know. Or co-ordinates, Map reference to Treasure Island."

I shrugged. "You two have damn all to do all day," I said. "Take copies and start thinking. Use your intuition."

It wasn't really true that they had nothing to do. In fact, they had all the boring work that Nathan and I begged out of on account of being in the field—collating the data we brought in, storing it in the computer, analyzing samples I picked up virtually everywhere I went—soil, crops, blood, and less pleasant things. Nobody really had so much free time that they could spend hours at a time staring at a row of figures and hoping for a blinding flash of insight. The wandering minstrel had hinted that his cronies had spent a good deal of *their* time working at the whole thing without any significant inspiration. The fact that they were ill-educated didn't really handicap them all that much. They knew the alphabet.

But Pete took a couple of copies anyhow. It didn't take long.

The airlock alarm sounded again, and Karen went to let Nathan in. He'd come back at my signal, to check with me before he went about the day's business.

"Your shadow keeping mine company?" I asked, as he came in.

He shook his head. "I rode out in the carriage," he said. "With Miranda. She's my guardian angel for today. We're going to Farina."

Farina was an island to the south, one of about forty in the archipelago that had a significant settlement. I'd only seen six so far, and Nathan had visited about the same number. If there were any dread secrets that Philip wanted kept, there were plenty of hiding places.

"Can you get some soil samples?" I asked him. "And sea-water close to the shore? The usual?"

He nodded. He leaned forward and picked up the paper from the table. He glanced at it idly, expecting it to be nothing worthy of his attention, but suddenly snatched it up in surprise.

"Where did you get this?" he demanded.

"That's what I wanted to tell you," I said. "The guy with the guitar playing in the market yesterday—he asked me to meet him last night. I got out of the house okay and met him in the cemetery. He gave me that—also a packet of some foul-tasting white powder. He's playing his cards close to his chest but I think there's something significant in it somewhere."

"I'll bet there is," he muttered, still looking at the numbers. "Who is he?"

"He didn't give his name. But he's no friend of Philip's. I guess he's as close to opposition as we're likely to find. A bandit, maybe, or a rebel. Impossible to say what might be behind him."

"And you slipped out of the house in the early hours to meet him?"

"What was I supposed to do?" I asked. "Report him to the *gendarmes*?"

"It was a risk. If they find an excuse to get mad with us they might just take it, you know. We're not exactly popular. If they figure out a pretext to tell us to get the hell out we'll be in a difficult situation. If they only knew how much authority we don't have they might do it anyhow."

"They won't do that while they still think they stand a chance of persuading us that everything in the garden's roses," I said. "And besides which, they don't know. Nobody saw me. So tell me about the paper. What's it mean?"

"As to that," he said. "I haven't a clue. But what I have got is another copy of the puzzle."

He reached into his jacket and pulled out a very similar bit of paper. He gave them both to me and I compared them. They were both handwritten in black ink, but neither the writing nor the ink was the same. The only difference was that Nathan's copy had one more number on it. Just a pair of digits: 16.

"They obviously think you need more help," I said. "They've given you an extra one. Who was it?"

"Miranda," he answered, pensively.

That was a surprise. Miranda was one of the legions of cousins. Her surname wasn't Wildeblood, or even Zarnecki, but she seemed well in, especially with Zarnecki. She seemed to have been assigned to Nathan in much the same way that Elkanah had been assigned to me—something which seemed to me to be monumentally unfair. Not only was she one of the masters while Elkanah was a servant but she was pretty and he was not. They seemed to have an altogether mistaken idea of the relative status of myself and Nathan.

"Why would Miranda be passing you bits of coded message?" I asked.

"The obvious answer," he said, "is that she wants the key to the code. That, after all, is what she asked me, in her guileless fashion."

"Didn't she tell you what it was or why she was asking? Hell, she must have said *something*."

Nathan shook his head. "She treated it as if it were a game. A kind of coquettish challenge. I thought it *was* a game. Something silly. Now I'm not so sure."

"Zarnecki put her up to it," I said. It was just an opinion formed out of prejudice. But I would have backed it with money.

"But why?" he said. "If your man doesn't know the key, it can't be *his* secret message. And if Zarnecki doesn't have the key, it can't be *his*. So whose is it? Or who's lying to us?"

"*Everybody*'s lying to us," I said tiredly. "Leave the damn thing until you've a spare moment. It may be important, it may be just something stupid—hell, it may even be a device to distract us. I'm going to concentrate on the package. That I can handle."

Nathan took back his copy of the conundrum, and returned to more mundane considerations.

"What did you promise this man you met?" he asked.

"Not a thing," I assured him. "I was the perfect diplomat."

"Is he dangerous?"

"How would I know? Dangerous to whom? That's a stupid question if ever there was one!"

He didn't seem offended. He was too preoccupied to be offended. "You're going to be aboard all day?" he asked. I nodded in reply, and he turned to Karen. "Are you going out?"

"Later maybe," she said. "When my shift ends."

"Be careful," he said.

She shrugged, but he wouldn't let it go.

"I mean it," he said. "There's something in the air. Things are beginning to happen. They're making moves. They aren't going to stick a knife in your back—yet. But be careful."

"Something is rotten in the State of . . ." she said, sarcastically.

He didn't reply. But they were both right. Something *was* rotten in this pretty little dictatorship which seemed to be working so well. I felt it. I knew it. There *had* to be something rotten . . . it wouldn't be natural otherwise. If there's one thing

25

we'd learned so far it was that all worlds had little surprises up their sleeves—for the colonies, for us.

"James Wildeblood must have been one hell of a clever bastard," I commented, letting the stream of thought carry me on. "To take over a colony from scratch, come to total dominance, and establish a historical pattern that could hold perfectly for over a century. And he did it all in 33 years."

"Well," said Karen, "if anyone can figure out how, it ought to be you. On the survey team, he had *your* job."

It was intended to be a simple nasty crack. But it was also true. It was a joke that pleased them all— Nathan, Karen . . . even Conrad. James Wildeblood and me. Evolutionary ecologists both. Ecologists and biochemists. He'd had experience like mine, a job not too dissimilar to mine.

And he'd also built an empire. Not to mention founding a dynasty.

You just can't tell what kind of potential some people have.

3

I spent most of the day tracking the sample carefully through the standard series of analytical tests and a few extra ones. It was a complicated molecule belonging to a class of biological products not uncommon on Poseidon—prevalent, in fact, throughout the life-system. It was a kind of supersteroid. Simpler molecules in the group were used by the local organisms as reservoir molecules for nutrient storage, the more complex ones were usually physiologically active as hormones or as catalytic fellow-travellers in enzymic manufactory processes. My specimen was one of the largest molecules of the family, about eighty-percent pure—most of the pollutants being breakdown debris. Whatever process had been used to extract and isolate it had also knocked it about a little bit. That was only to be expected. The colony had nothing that could hold the faintest candle to the *Daedalus* lab. They were pretty clever to get eighty-percent—but then, James Wildeblood had been the man for the job.

Because it was such a large molecule the procedures took time. They practically ate up the day. It wasn't exactly strenuous work but don't ever let anyone tell you that computer-aided analysis with automatic measurement at every stage is labor-saving. It may save your fingers and it's freed us forever from the embarrassment of the pipette, but you need eyes like a hawk and a brain in overdrive if you hope to keep up. I always tried to keep up—in the course of a couple of thousand mechanical

27

operations *something* always slips a cog, and if you don't catch it as and when you might as well start all over.

I missed the midday meal, but managed to extract myself in the early evening. Karen had been out to soak in a little fresh air (perhaps a little too fresh, as the unseasonal cold spell was still going strong) and had gotten back without having had a knife stuck in her back, despite Nathan's premonitions.

"Well?" she said. "Cracked it wide open?"

"Making progress," I told her. "I'm between experiments. I now know what it is."

"But not . . ."

". . . what it does. No. That's the tricky one."

"Have you enough of the stuff to let you find out?" put in Pete. "There didn't look to be a vast quantity."

"Plenty," I assured him. "My equipment could run a million operations on a teaspoonful. It's just time . . . I'll have to trace its physiological activity through the whole series of tissue cultures. Couldn't lend me a couple of milliliters of fresh blood, by any chance?"

"Use your own," he said—somewhat ungraciously, I thought.

"I'd lend them to you with pleasure," said Karen, "only I'd be very apprehensive about getting them back. I dread to think what unholy things go on behind that closed door."

"Ah well," I muttered, philosophically, "if you can't spare it. . . ."

"What do you *think* it does?" asked Pete, steering the conversation away from a topic he found mildly distasteful.

"At a guess," I said, "it boosts the bastards into orbit. Poseidon's answer to the joys of spring. Or Wildeblood's answer, I should say."

"A narcotic?"

"Not in the literal sense of the word. Nor an ataractic. A psychotropic of some kind, though. Has to be. But moderately safe—it doesn't impair the faculties or seriously endanger health. At the worst it accelerates the metabolism and shortens the lifespan somewhat, along with altering the chemical balance of the tissues in what seems to be a fairly haphazard manner."

"That's a pretty detailed guess," he said.

I shrugged. "This drug isn't listed in the survey team's report. It's a biological product but it's not there. Why not? James Wildeblood was on that survey team doubling as ecologist and biochemist. He omitted it—and not by accident. He came back here with the colony, as a member of the executive, and within a decade he *was* the executive. Is it too much to believe that he had a trick up his sleeve and that this innocent white powder—or guilty white powder—is it? I reckon that he took over the colony by putting each and every member of it on a set of puppet strings."

"He hooked them?" This from Karen.

"That's what I think," I confirmed. "As for the rest of the guess—well, I've examined quite a number of the colonists more or less at random. It seems only reasonable to assume that some of the slight anomalies I've measured are attributable to the drug—and, as an inevitable corollary—that the lack of any major anomalies means that the drug is relatively harmless. It probably breaks down pretty quickly in the body—I've never found it in a blood sample, although I've picked up some molecules which I now know to be its breakdown products. See?"

"You ever get tired of being such a hot-shot?" asked Karen.

I ignored her. "It's all being checked out," I said,

aiming my face at Pete, who'd asked the original question. "I'll leave things set overnight and come back tomorrow. I have a feeling, though, that all the mass of data I'm getting will turn out like the proverbial statistical bikini."

"What's a proverbial statistical bikini?" asked Pete. I glanced at Karen. She was dying to know but didn't want to ask.

"Some anonymous wit once coined a phrase," I said. "Statistics are like the two halves of a bikini. What they reveal is interesting but what they leave concealed is vital."

It didn't get its usual grudging laugh. I guess it's a rather esoteric joke.

"So okay," said Karen, sarcastically. "How come your research magnificent is going the same way?"

"By tomorrow," I said, "I'll have the thing labelled and all its multifarious properties isolated. I'll have measured its chemical and physiological activities to the fifth significant figure. But what I still won't know is what Cyrano de Bergerac originally charged me with finding out."

"Which is?"

"Where it comes from. Its chemical cousins are scattered far and wide in everything which grows or crawls on this planet's face. I can't even make a respectable guess as to whether it's plant or animal. All I know is that it's from someplace Wildeblood looked. I'll search his survey reports for a suspicious hole, but I'll lay odds I won't find one. He'll have covered his tracks perfectly."

"And so," said Karen, "the big question remains unanswered. So what *have* we got?"

"Not a lot," I said. "Let's see what Nathan can make of it. If anyone can make capital out of it, he can. One of Philip's secrets is a secret no more, at any rate. And, of course, there is the general pragmatic point."

"What's that?" she asked.

"Well," I said, "we now know how to become emperors. Pick our planet, and we can take it over. We could even have one each, or maybe a little galactic empire."

Pete's mouth was open a little, though he knew it wasn't serious.

"Let's you and me invade Earth," suggested Karen. "I have this plan, see, for setting the world to rights . . ."

"Not Earth," I said, shaking my head sadly.

"Why not?"

"Problems of supply," I said. "Also demand. Earth is suffering from a surfeit of puppet-strings already. It has to be a colony—a virgin colony. I doubt if we could take over this one at such a late stage, unless we actually took over Philip's source of supply. Starting up our own factory in opposition would just lead to all-out war. We'd have to be there at the very beginning, just like James Wildeblood."

"Wildeblood and Machiavelli and Alexander the Great," muttered Karen.

"Wait a second," said Pete. "That isn't so funny, you know."

"You mean you *want* to hitch yourself to a new colony and become a dictator?" I said, still not serious, though a little thought echoed in the back of my mind that it wasn't so inconceivable, and if that was what he did want—or Karen, or Nathan—then maybe it wasn't so funny. . . .

But that wasn't what he meant.

"No," he said. "Not my scene. What I mean is: if, here and now, somebody started up in opposition to Philip . . . leading to all-out war. Why do you think the guy that gave you the drug wants to know where it comes from? Think for a minute."

I thought. It didn't really need a minute. It was

obvious. Only sometimes, when your mind's full and buzzing, you can overlook the obvious.

"If this drug is the secret of Philip's power-base," I said, returning to the safety of "if" because we were dealing with reality again, "then any opposition, to be meaningful opposition, would need to know it. And once they did. . . ."

We'd come to find out how the colony was doing, to give it a helping hand. We were supposed to be working in the interests of the whole population. But how do you do that? How do you work in *everybody*'s interest, when you find a divided society, masters and servants—controllers and controlled—at its crudest level, maybe pushers and junkies. How do you walk into the middle of a game of chess, or an all-in brawl and say: "Right, folks, we're here to make things better for *everyone*."

No wonder Philip was worried about us, and having us followed, and keeping his secrets. Our declared intention was to overcome any little problems the people might have . . . like, for instance, addiction to some local joy-juice. How was he to know how we'd react when we found out? Come to that, even *I* wasn't sure how we were going to react when we found out. I knew how I felt, but what, if anything, was I going to do? And as for Nathan, I had my suspicions about which way his perverted thinking might run, but I couldn't be sure.

The future was still hazy, but it seemed to me then that if I could find out where the drug came from—if I *did*—then there were three alternatives. We could pat Philip on the back, say: "Jolly good show, wonderful colony you're building here," and leave him to it. Or we could let the cat out of the bag and start a war. Or we could go to Philip and say: "Look here, old boy, we don't quite approve of the way you go about things—how about giving up virtually everything you've got, just as a kindly gesture." Three alternatives, take your pick. And while we were picking. . . .

As Nathan said, there was something in the air. We were coming late into the game and *they*'d already begun to make their moves.

We sat around like the three wise monkeys, contemplating the ghastliness of it all. Then Karen said: "Where does your stupid number-code fit into all this?"

"I wish I knew," I replied. I repeated it, for effect.

Not only were they making their moves . . . but they were making moves we didn't even understand.

"Suppose you're right," said Pete. "Suppose the whole damn colony *is* addicted to this stuff. Could you break the addiction? Could you, shall we say, restore the balance of nature."

"Sure," I said. "That's a party trick. But the point is—would they want me to? This stuff doesn't constitute a hold because of the threat of withdrawal symptoms—it constitutes a hold because it has something to sell. It's not the fact that they need it that constitutes the problem . . . it's the fact that they want it. It must pack one hell of a belt if it let Wildeblood take over so completely so easily. The fight isn't about whether they want the stuff or not but over who controls its production and distribution . . . *their* fight, that is. I'm not quite sure what *our* fight is about. Maybe we ought to be looking to break the addiction for good and all. Maybe we oughtn't. You know the line Nathan will take."

"The colony is successful," said Karen, quoting what she presumed would be Nathan's thinking. "Anything which has contributed to that success is *ipso facto* a Good Thing. J. Wildeblood, biochemist and dictator, gets a medal, and the drug gets a round of applause. Maybe he's right, don't look at me like that, Alex. If the seeds of cynicism haven't germinated in you yet it isn't because they haven't been planted. It's because they fell among the weeds of idealism. You know the world isn't perfect; you know we always have to settle for what we can get. If this is what we can get ... isn't it better than Dendra? Isn't it better than Kilner's colonies?"

The situation on Dendra had been pretty bad. The colonies that Kilner had recontacted on the first *Daedalus* mission had found more than their share of troubles. Pietrasante had told me that I had to share my authority with Nathan because his precious committees believed that the problems weren't primarily ecological problems of co-adaptation but social problems of people not being able to form viable communities. Maybe from Pietrasante's point of view—and Nathan's—Wildeblood had found the answer. How to conquer a world ... the operative word being "conquer".

"Maybe I don't have the stomach for this job," I said. "I swallowed Dendra. Maybe I'll even sit silently by while Nathan rigs the books on that one in the name of political convenience. But how many more do I have to swallow?"

They didn't answer me.

Kilner, my predecessor, had returned to Earth a very bitter man. He had let his bitterness run over, and had turned in a report which said, none too subtly, that mankind wasn't fit to go out to the stars, that the colonies couldn't work and ought to be abandoned. I thought that no matter what happened I couldn't follow the same intellectual course. I thought that my own faith in extraterrestrial expansion was utterly unshakable. Now, for the first time, I began to wonder. The kind of thing that I kept having to face wasn't what I'd expected. I'm an ecologist, and ecological problems have ready-made answers, involving harmony and balance. Nature red in tooth and claw, maybe, but flexible nature, manipulable nature. Genetic engineering had given us the means to *find* solutions to ecological problems. But social ecology was different. Behavioral engineering we not only didn't have but didn't want. The human being was still sacred. We still believed in evil. Me too. Me, perhaps, more than most.

"A moment ago," I said, "I was joking. I said that we'd just discovered a recipe for empire. It was just a throwaway remark. But maybe it isn't so ridiculous. Can we really have that much confidence in one another? How about Nathan? He's a politician. . . . It's the kind of power he deals in. If I find out where this drug comes from, and how to refine it . . . that's power. I go ahead and do things like that—analyze things and find out where they come from—because I'm interested, because I want to know. But I shouldn't shut my eyes to the fact that, seen through other eyes, what I'm doing is discovering potential sources of political power. Should I?"

"You've got your empire," said Karen. "It's in your head and in your lab. Pete has his . . . we're sitting inside it. Nathan doesn't want a world of his own, to manipulate and play with like a toy."

"Wildeblood did," I answered.

"And how about you?" The question came from Pete, and it was directed at Karen. It wasn't the kind of question I could imagine Pete asking. Karen, yes . . . as a snide assault on somebody else's vanity. But coming from Karen you could ignore a remark like that as so much froth. Aimed at Karen, from Pete, it was different. Maybe he'd taken uncharacteristic offence at her offhand dismissal of his own imperial limitations.

"I've got everything I need," she replied, with some asperity.

Maybe it wasn't true. But I knew that whatever she wanted, it wasn't a Wildeblood set-up. She even found it inconceivable that Nathan should want such a thing, and I wasn't so sure that *I* found that particular notion inconceivable.

But the argument wasn't getting us anywhere. Turning it on one another was really only a way of turning it away from the real focal points: Wildeblood, Philip, and the guitar-playing Cyrano.

"There's no point having a row," I said. "We can have a much bigger and better one next time Nathan's here. We very probably will. So let's drop it now. I'm going back to work until Conrad checks in. Call me when he does, okay?"

Without any seeming effort, they cast the tension aside.

"Sure," said Pete. "Don't bleed yourself to death."

"And don't conjure up the devil by mistake," added Karen.

I promised that I wouldn't. But my propensity for metaphor couldn't resist making me ask myself whether perhaps I already had.

4

What kind of man was Wildeblood?

A scientist . . . my kind?

My kind, then . . . a man stranded somewhere in middle age. Stranded, too, in a maze. A maze of ideas. We'd live, he and I, in a world that is totally alien to common man (Nathan, say—without deliberate insult) or mechanical man (Pete), or even alien man (Mariel, with alienating talent). *Everybody* lives in a world in which the raw data—sensory impressions—are organized into an inordinately complex web of fictions. The extent to which we are different from one another is the extent to which our fictions—our ways of seeing, of making sense of what we see, our ways of believing and knowing and making sense of those too—are our own. That, of course, is a matter of degree. "We" is a very flexible term: mankind, nation, group, you and I, myself plus hypothetical other. So . . . what fictions do I share with Wildeblood? When we see living things, we see them as complex chemical machines. When we see worlds we see them as systems. Our view of the living world is reified, systematized. We deal with problems of incalculable complexity, and we tend to translate everything into those kind of problems. We feed like gluttonous vampires on the lifeblood of logic. Life, ordinary and everyday, moment and universe, is displayed thus in our consciousness. Our aims? Solutions. Answers. More and more and more of them. An infinity of conclusions jumped, Q. E. D.'s, eurekas.

We experience the world, it is said (and "we" is here at its most flexible) as a continual process of culmination and disintegration, order-implicit-in-chaos in self-identifying ambivalence. We rejoice in culminations, and find there pleasure, joy and love, while the counterpoints of hatred and fear relate to the inevitable forces of opposition—disintegration.

Wildeblood and I, scientists, hate and fear questions, love and take pleasure in answers. Riddles *versus* solutions. An artificial world, certainly. A world of ideative fictions. But so are they all.

Except . . . that Wildeblood had wanted something more than I. He had wanted an empire. He had planned it, and he had made it. Scientifically.

Where was the difference—the *essential* difference—between Wildeblood and I?

It had to lie, I think, in attitudes to people. Other people, in my world-view, are somewhat exempt from the perspectives I apply to the living world, to living systems in general. They fall into a different conceptual category. A special one. One which I can unashamedly label "sacred."

But it had not been so for Wildeblood. Wildeblood had seen people in the same fictive light which had, for him, illuminated the whole universe. People, in Wildeblood's imagination, were reified, systematized. Elements in problems, as generalized and as symbolic as a row of algebraic x's. To be manipulated. To be organized. To be *solved*.

That was what Wildeblood's empire really was. The solution to a problem which James Wildeblood had discovered or invented within his mind. This was the way to put it into perspective.

James Wildeblood had come to Poseidon with the survey team. He had looked at the world and found it good.

He found a world which had dilute oceans covering four-fifths of its surface. Of the remaining fifth the greater part was useless because of an un-happy geological circumstance. The elevated rocks were eccentric conglomerates which, to put it crudely, leaked rather badly. The water table of the continental masses tended to be very deep, and rainfall seeped through the surface very quickly. There were few rivers and fewer lakes—the interior of each large land mass was an arid waste, the rain which fell there returning to the sea by subterranean ways. But the small fraction of the land surface which remained—a few island chains and a few verdant areas close to the continental coasts—was promising indeed.

The soil was rich in many places, and would support Earthly crops well. And if the local vegetable produce had little to offer in the way of useful comestibles, that deficit was more than made up by the bounty of the sea. The sea was green with algae—not the cloying weeds of Floria's inshore waters but a rich soup of unicellular species, abundantly spiced with protozoa and complex micro-organisms of all kinds. Over the entire surface of the ocean there was a stratum of plankton some two to ten fathoms deep, which could be dredged and dried to form a nutritious (if somewhat vapid) food in its own right, and which in addition supported great numbers of fish and a host of other creatures, many species of which were eminently edible.

With such resources Poseidon was obviously ripe for colonization despite the relatively limited usable land surface. The question the surveyors had to ask was whether there was, in the local life-system, anything which might prove inimical to human life. The answering of that question had been largely Wildeblood's responsibility. He had convinced himself that the world was perfectly safe. And, it seemed, he had been right.

But it also seemed that in the process of the investigation he had made other discoveries—significant ones—which he had most carefully excluded from his reports.

He had looked at the world, found it good, and decided that it should be his. . . .

It was not unheard-of for members of successful survey teams to volunteer for the colonies that were to be detached thereto. They were allowed—and, in fact, given every encouragement—to do so. The UN might lose top-flight scientists, but the colonies gained the services of men who already knew the world as intimately as was possible and who also had faith in it. The fact that a member of a survey team was willing to go out with the colony was straightforward testimony to the fact that the surveyors had confidence in their recommendations.

And so, Wildeblood returned to Poseidon, already the most important member of the colony, but supposedly as an advisor rather than a leader. He was the man to whom the colonists would bring their problems—a wise man, in many ways a paternal figure, a man people would trust and on whom they would inevitably rely for guidance. But Wildeblood had not been satisfied with that. And he had known the world rather more intimately than anyone supposed.

Two of the colonies that Kilner had visited had had members of the original survey teams attached to their initial executive bodies. What difference it had made to their chances it was, by the time Kilner came, impossible to judge. The colonies had done badly. Perhaps, without the survey men and their expertise they would have done even worse. Perhaps not. Similarly, it was difficult now to weigh up the positive side of Wildeblood's contribution to the Poseidon colony. Perhaps, in his absence, it would have done as well. Perhaps, if he had been content to advise and assist a more democratic government, it would have done as well.

But on the other hand, perhaps not.

Now, more than a hundred years later, Poseidon—or Wildeblood, as it had become and as it truly *was*—was still ruled by one man and a small family group: Philip Wildeblood the second and his acknowledged cousins. Whether it is semantically correct to call Philip a tyrant and his government a totalitarian one I am not sure. His was no reign of overt terror, the force he used being subtle and even invisible. But I thought of it as tyranny, and if I were to be proved right about the steroid drug then I would be utterly confirmed in that conviction.

The colony thrived. It had a larger population than any other colony so far recontacted. Its technological progress compared well with Floria's. (It boasted no locomotives, but its communicative problems were rather different. It had guns, but again, this arose from a difference in manifest priorities. One could not say that either world was "more advanced"—their achievements were roughly comparable, taking into account social differences and environmental requirements.) There was a high degree of specialization among individuals and communities. Oil and coal measures were being worked on the nearest continent, south of the island chain which still remained the heart of the colony. Conditions on the continents were not inviting, and the mines, at least, were kept supplied with labor largely thanks to the penal system. Manufacturing was largely the prerogative of the islands nearer the mainland. The large island from which the colony was administered, called Jensen island, was the center of the shipbuilding industry, but also boasted a great deal of arable land and was

41

the most heavily cultivated of all the islands although its neighbors to the north-east were exclusively given over to agricultural development. It all seemed to work, and the plan by which it *did* work was almost entirely the legacy of James Wildeblood. He had designed the administrative hierarchy, the legal system, the penal system, and plotted the likely course of industrial progress. He had ordained the educational methods and priorities (giving a very high priority to practical considerations) and, unlike the Planners of Floria, had not found it necessary to keep a desperately tight control over who could know what. Anyone could take the trouble to learn anything he had a mind to—but he could only *use* what James Wildeblood had prescribed for his use. Very few people tried to step outside their allotted roles, it seemed, and no one succeeded.

The lack of conflict, I thought, had to be a clue to the fact that rebellion was impossible. And it was impossible not because it was unthinkable (as the Planners had tried—and failed—to make it on Floria) but because it was impractical. I suspected it was because there could be no real question of *independence* on Poseidon/Wildeblood. Everyone was dependent—on the drug, and on the government. That was the way it had to be.

And that, my investigations into the properties of the white powder informed me, was very probably the way it *was*.

So much for James Wildeblood, scientist and Utopian (for the colony was a Utopia, all right—for the man on top).

But there was more to the planet than the colony. Perhaps there was more to the whole situation than the colony. Certainly we had priorities here above and beyond the scope of our missions on Floria and Dendra. Because Poseidon also had intelligent life.

Poseidon had no mammals, no birds, and no reptiles. Its life-system had never invested in the evolution of the cleidoic egg. And, indeed, there had been little enough incentive for it to do so. So little of the land surface could possibly provide a viable habitat for animals of any considerable size, and virtually all of it was within spitting distance of the sea.

Thus, the so-called "higher animals" of Poseidon—the "next step up" from the fishes—belonged exclusively to a group which we must needs call the amphibians.

They resembled Earthly amphibians in the one important respect that at certain times of their life-cycle they breathed water, and at other times air. In many other ways, too, they were often reminiscent. The largest group, nicknamed "whaleys" by the survey team (perhaps by Wildeblood himself), looked for all the world like giant bloated newts. The land-going phase of the intelligent species and its near relatives could be conveniently imagined as a bipedal salamander (and, true to form, they had been dubbed "salamen"—a term I hated but was constrained to use). All the species laid eggs in colossal batches, underwater, and dressed in sheaths of gel which both protected the eggs and provided the new-born with their vital sustenance during the first few days. Very few specimens of this spawn had ever been discovered, and it was presumed that the larger species deposited it in special breeding grounds, almost certainly in subterranean caves.

But we must, as always, beware of these inviting comparisons and by the habits of nomenclature which inevitably attend them. For if the amphibians of Poseidon were in some ways reminiscent of

Earthly forms, they were also—in some very important respects—crucially different.

On Earth, the amphibians flourished as a group very briefly, and then went the way of all flesh, into mass-extinction for the majority of species and evolutionary backwaters for the survivors. They were outshone in the evolutionary narrative by the reptiles—who, in their turn, were overtaken as heroes of the drama by the mammals and the birds.

But on Poseidon, the day of the amphibians never ended, extending through far greater numbers of millennia and eras. Whereas the Earthly groups had been obliterated or sidetracked the Poseidon families had continued to evolve. Chance had innovated, natural selection had refined. And a route to intelligence rather different from that followed by the life-system of Earth had been discovered.

There are basically two prerequisites for the evolution of intelligence. One is that the species concerned should be able to develop and carry a brain of sufficient magnitude. Large brains are mechanically viable only for bipeds and for creatures of the sea—at least so far as creatures with "heads" (brain-boxes equipped with arrays of sensors) are concerned. Thus, on Earth intelligence developed to the highest degree in a species of primate that walked erect and a few aquatic species (dolphins and the misnamed killer whales). The other prerequisite is that the species concerned should have a life-cycle into which the learning process may be incorporated. This is a complex factor, involving such things as the capacity for parental influence on the young (greatest, on Earth, in mammal species, because mammals suckle their young) and the mechanical and behavioral capacity of the individual to put learning to good *use* (hence the priority on limbs adaptable as tools ... a lack which put a limit on dolphin evolution). Where these mechanical and behavioral potentials exist along with the capacity for parental influence, evolution will tend to cater for these potentials by encouraging neoteny—the prolongation of the developmental phase of the individual and exposure of the developing organism to external influences, and hence to the acquisition of highly flexible adaptive responses to a wide range of environmental stimuli.

Now, the amphibians of Poseidon had these prerequisites in what can only be described as remarkable abundance. One phase of their life-cycle was lived under water, the other, in the case of certain medium-sized "salamanders," proved amenable to an erect position using the tail as an extra support.

In the cultivation of such an erect posture the upper limbs were freed (and in the aquatic phases these same limbs were the relatively unfunctional— unfunctional so far as locomotion is concerned— forelimbs) for mechanical development as "hands." (This potential can still be seen in Earthly newts, which have webbed "fingers" on their forelimbs very similar to human hands.)

What they lacked, principally, was the degree of parental care which was, on Earth, a necessary encouragement to the evolution of mammal intelligence. Their eggs, though provided with a slightly greater measure of protection than the eggs of the fish from which they had evolved, were still produced in vast quantities, on the assumption that the young must suffer a tremendous mortality rate in their early stages. There was little or no potential in the behavior-patterns of the amphibians to encourage evolutionary modification of this kind of reproductive pattern.

But the amphibians had a trick up their sleeve.

On Earth, mammalian parental care had paved the way for the evolution of neoteny in the potentially-intelligent primates. On Poseidon, the amphibians already *had* a kind of neoteny, and this was what permitted them to work the trick in reverse.

On Earth, there is a neotenic amphibian called the axolotl. Its juvenile form, equipped with gills, may, under different sets of circumstances, *either* metamorphose into an air-breathing salamander (the "normal" adult/reproductive phase) *or* remain an aquatic creature equipped with gills and develop reproductive organs as such. This *choice* of whether or not to metamorphose is genetically transmitted by either reproductive process.

In the days when the first terrestrial species had appeared on Poseidon, they too had found this faculative metamorphosis a useful device. But while, on Earth, the axolotl remained an evolutionary freak, the amphibians of Poseidon went in for this curious brand of developmental ambiguity in a big way. It became the key to their evolution of developmental flexibility, which opened the door to intelligence.

The largest species—the whaleys and their kindred—did not practice neoteny. Their juvenile forms, in growing vast, had to metamorphose into air-breathers. To be as big as a whale you have to breathe air. Gills can't cope.

The smallest species, too, did not go in much for the protracted juvenile stage—anything smaller than, say, a rat found little dividend in it, although one or two species could work the trick.

In the medium range, the species which characteristically weighed, when mature, something between a kilo and a hundred kilos, found neoteny useful. They had to go carefully on land, always in danger of desication and—being cold-blooded—always at the mercy of the weather. It was convenient to keep a reservoir of breeders perpetually at sea.

But it was at the top of the medium range that the potential really lay, for it was here that the potential existed for big brains and hands, along with the kind of mechanical aptitude that something as big as a whale—or even a cow—simply doesn't have because of excessive overall bulk. Here were the species who could really use neoteny in more ways than one. In these species there was an evolutionary boom. The salamen developed rudimentary temperature control, and evolved physiologically towards a pseudomammalian internal environment. And they developed metamorphic choice into a fine art with one fairly simple modification—they kept their choices open both ways.

The juveniles hatched out in the sea, probably—as I've said—in underwater caves. There they fell prey to fish and all manner of invertebrate carnivores. But enough survived to grow, and ultimately the pre-reproductive aquatic forms would join a herd made up partly of others like themselves and partly of mature aquatic forms with reproductive potential. Then, having learned something of what life in the underwater herd had to teach them, they might either metamorphose into terrestrial forms—still pre-reproductive—or into mature aquatic forms. The mature aquatic forms still retained the potential to metamorphose into mature terrestrial forms, while the juvenile terrestrial forms could go on through a new developmental phase before either developing into mature terrestrials *or* undergoing remetamorphosis into juvenile aquatic form.

And so, *ad infinitum*. Or, to be precise, until death caught up. Mature terrestrial forms could always back-metamorphose into mature aquatic phase. The only switch which couldn't happen was that no mature reproductive morph could metamorphose (or de-develop) into a juvenile phase. Outside that, no changes were barred. And the potential existed for virtually limitless prolongation of the developmental stage, for as long as that was adaptively productive. . . .

Mature individuals and juveniles mingled on both land and sea, and varied between themselves as to their experiential histories. It was complex, and maybe untidy. Maybe God could have arranged things a little more simply if he hadn't been prepared to let natural selection do so much of the work. But then, maybe he could have made a better job of us, too—we don't quite measure up to any standards of aesthetic perfection no matter how hard we pretend.

The thing was, that the Poseidon pattern worked. The salamen had intelligence. They communicated with one another by signs (no other way is convenient for both land *and* underwater). They made use of tools, of clothing. They always operated in groups, co-operating in virtually all endeavors. There was a constant exchange of materials between the part of the tribe that was on land and the part in the sea, which made things easier for both groups. Whenever the proportions got out of balance there would be a consciously ordained metamorphosis by selected members of the larger group to adjust the balance.

And so it went.

This was the aspect of Poseidon which seemed to me far more interesting and more important than Wildeblood's empire. I would rather have been with Conrad and Linda and Mariel, trying out Mariel's talent for the first time in the circumstances where it *might*—only might—prove itself of incalculable value.

At that particular time, Wildeblood's empire and the salamen seemed worlds apart. But they weren't. And that was the chief reason why I was at base, working with Nathan, trying to assess the potential of the colony.

Because one of the questions we had to answer was a long-term question. What happened, or was to happen, when the expanding human population met up, in a meaningful way, with the salamen? It hadn't happened yet. The colony was wrapped up in its own affairs. In a hundred years and more Wildeblood's progeny had ignored the aliens completely.

But there had to come a time. . . .

And, bearing in mind that the colony was what Wildeblood had made it, what kind of meeting would it be?

It was a question that worried me. It was a question which, when I thought about James Wildeblood, and Philip, and Zarnecki, also frightened me.

5

"We're getting things done," reported Conrad. "We've been working from the base, mapping a region about five miles square and taking census. There are two groups of salamen near to us at the present time. They see us wandering about and they don't appear to be hostile. They watch us from a distance—and for the moment we're not ostentatiously watching back. We'll probably try to make contact with the nearer group, which is slightly larger in any case."

"How's Mariel?" I asked.

"She's fine. She hasn't really been close to them, yet, but she says that she'd know already if there was anything like the kind of disturbance which hit her on Dendra. She says their minds are strange enough not to wrench at hers. We're taking things pretty easy but I trust her."

"No observations yet on the language?"

"Not the real language. We've seen them making signs but until they get used to us we aren't going to start systematic watching and cataloguing. We hear them, though. I guess you can't call the sounds they make a language, but they have a small range of whistles and barks to supplement the signs. Obviously this is something unique to the terrestrials. Mariel wants to get going, though—she's impatient with mapping."

"What do they look like?"

"The tallest ones stand about five and a half feet, but even the smallest—the juveniles—are four-ten. They don't do a lot of growing in the terrestrial phase, though they change somewhat in physique and body coloring. Their skins look rather like plastic from a distance—smooth, with a kind of marbled effect—but I think they're probably softer than they look. They virtually all wear things like ponchos, made from vegetable fiber. Sometimes, in hot sun, they use headgear made out of big, spatulate leaves. Their heads look big by human standards, but not really frog-like . . . more like seals. In bright sunlight their skins look very dark—black dappled brown and green, but when the day's overcast the green stands out more, and when they're in the desert areas the brown seems more obvious, though how profound a change in the actual skin pigmentation there is I'm not entirely sure. The juveniles are generally much lighter in tone, with the black reduced to powder-blue in the youngest ones. I don't know yet whether they have distinctive individual patterns that will allow us to tell them apart. I can't spot any significant element which will even allow us to tell members of the one group from members of the other."

"What's the situation between the two groups?"

"Keep pretty much to themselves. Basically peaceful. They pass by one another in narrow gullies without reaching for their knives. All the adults carry stone tools about with them, although there's a much larger stock in continuous production and use at the village. But they seem to use them on crabs and trees, not on each other. But this is the good season coming up. When winter comes and things get tough . . . then there might be a bit more aggression in interpersonal relationships."

"What about the mating season?" I asked. "It should be now or pretty soon. Any signs of activity within the groups?"

"Not a lot," he replied. "Maybe they're waiting for the weather to cheer up. I would if I were them. There's a certain amount of tension within the groups—we've seen squabbles, especially between juveniles. But until we get a lot closer we won't be able to make any genuine judgments about what goes on in the village. They do have privacy, you know—the lodges are spaced and they put a lot of ingenuity into the business of improvising shelters. There are some aspects of their lives we might never get to know much about. And they don't come around trying to peep into our tents."

"They don't show a lot of curiosity, then? Do you think they recognize you as intelligent beings?"

"I don't know. If one appears in the camp, raises his palm, and says 'I come in peace' I'll call you promptly and let you know."

"And if he says 'Take me to your leader' you'll bring him right along?"

"Sure."

"I wish I was with you," I said.

"It's time the rest of us got an outing," he said, with mock sourness. "You've had all the fun before. How's the routine coming along?"

"Slowly," I said. "As might be expected with only one of me. And with people always looking over my shoulder ... not to mention the extracurricular activities." I gave him an abridged account of the meeting in the cemetery and my thoughts on the white powder. "How are you on codes and ciphers?" I finished up.

"A past master," he assured me.

I read him the number sequence, adding in the extra one that had been on Nathan's copy. "There's a prize for decoding it," I said, "but we haven't decided what it is yet."

"The message or the prize?"

"Both."

"There's not much *of* it," he complained.

"It's never easy," I reminded him.

"If it was in a Sunday paper," he mused, "I could be sure that there was enough, and that the solution would be simple, elegant and adequately clued. But something tells me that I'd be taking a lot for granted if I approached this on the same basis."

"I think they're being parsimonious with their handouts," I said. "Basically, they want the answer but they don't want us to have the whole message, just in case it's anything interesting. It's called having your cake and eating it too."

"Well," said Conrad. "If we're going to be decoding an alien sign-language next week I guess a little practice should just about tune us up. It shouldn't defeat us, if we can spare the time to think about it. Don't happen to know who wrote it or why or what they might have wanted to communicate so cunningly?"

"Not yet," I said. "But I might get some clues next time my cloak-and-dagger man gives me a whisper. I take it, incidentally, that you're having no problems on your end with . . . shall we say, overbearing solicitude on the part of our hosts?"

"No. The boss man is a pleasant enough type, and he doesn't interfere with our affairs. Nor do his servants. They stick pretty much to camp and even help out a bit. They're keeping an eye on us, of course, but not obtrusively and not with the true obsessiveness of the paranoid. The ship's not here at the moment—it's picking up supplies for us and should be back in three days. But the sailors are no trouble either. They didn't even steal anything except a few small items of no particular significance. If they wanted to, they could make things impossible for us . . . but they don't. They're okay."

"I only wish I could say the same about our end," I commented dryly. "Um . . . given that they don't interfere, would you say that they might prove ... talkative, given the appropriate encouragement."

"Our guardian angel, never. Nor the servants ... they're tight-lipped by nature. The ship's crew, certainly. But we're not exactly encouraged to mingle, and they don't look to make friends with us. There's a kind of social gulf, if you know what I mean. Possibly the captain or one of his officers, but I don't really think that we're ideally placed as spies."

"No," I agreed. "It was only a thought. If you do happen to hear a careless word dropped.... There seems to be this feeling abroad that one hell of a lot is going on that we don't know about. Yet."

"We've been down four weeks," said Conrad. "We're strangers—outsiders. I know places on Earth where you get the cold shoulder if your grandfather wasn't born within a stone's throw. Take it easy. We'll make contact. It's probably a toss-up whether we make contact first with the aliens or the people. That's the way it is."

It was a note of optimism that might have come in handy, but I couldn't accept it. I was too far gone in gloom and suspicion. I signed off.

Pete was off-shift catching up with some sleep, but Karen was about, supposedly looking after the ship. It didn't need looking after—everything dangerous was switched off. But the checks still had to be carried out with ruthless efficiency. I made a couple of cups of coffee. I intended to go back to the house to sleep, as a matter of form, but I didn't see why I had to suffer their local brew as well. I didn't take my responsibilities as a guest quite as seriously as Nathan.

"See anything interesting today?" I asked, to make conversation. "While you were out?"

"There was a rather pleasant young man appeared—purely by coincidence, of course—to keep me company."

"They've got half a dozen people constantly watching the ship," I said. "They're on the hill in the cottages. And I think there's always a man in the coppice over the other way, watching our non-existent back door. They don't believe that the airlock is the only way out. Did he seduce you?"

"Who? Oh ... him. No. I didn't seduce him, either. There seemed to be little point. He looked as if he'd had practice."

"At what?"

"Being seduced. I don't think I'd have had the advantage of surprise."

"Maybe not," I conceded.

Silence fell. I didn't like it much, so I said something else. "The thing I can't figure out," I mused, "is how Wildeblood and company have managed to go more than a century without the secret of where they get the stuff—assuming it is their junk—leaking out. How do you keep a secret for a hundred years? At least a dozen people must be in on the whole thing, and hundreds must be in on the distribution. So how come Cyrano de Bergerac still needs me to tell him where the stuff comes from?"

"His intelligence network probably has an I.Q. of three," she said, tiredly. "You beat your brains out too much. Give it a rest."

"If I were living here," I said, "I'd find out. I wouldn't rest until I found out. One way or another...."

"The mines are probably full of people who thought the same," she said. "And likely the seabed too. Just be careful you don't end up in the same place. You wouldn't like hewing coal."

It was a warning I didn't take seriously.

Perhaps I should have.

6

When I got back to the house Nathan was playing cards with Zarnecki, Philip and Miranda. I was offered a game by Philip's sister, Alice, who volunteered to co-opt a man named Cade and some other relative whose name I didn't catch, who were presently employed playing some game that was obscenely like billiards in the next room. I declined. We played cards on the ship during transits, but there seemed to be something slightly decadent about playing cards with the in-group on a colony world. I didn't like passing the time as a way of life. In addition, there was the small matter of protocol. I didn't have to inquire who was winning in the game that was going already. No money was at stake but diplomatically-aided fortune smiled perpetually the same way, bringing her small bounty of joy and satisfaction.

Personally, I didn't see a lot of point in playing games with Philip.

I would have been quite happy to find something to do on my own account—or even to go straight to bed and catch up on some sleep. But our hosts were nothing if not dutiful. Alice felt compelled to look after me. She was younger than Philip, but not by much—he was getting on for thirty, and she was in her late twenties. There was another sibling—another sister, younger still—but she was away at one of the schools where the elite were taught.

After I'd refused food, Alice had to cast around a bit for another idea to offer. But she had, by now, some idea of what kind of person I was, and she'd obviously been keeping something back for just such an occasion. She asked me if I'd seen the west wing.

I hadn't. I hadn't seen much of the house at all—I'm not a great one for touring vast, half-empty houses oozing a lousy hundred years of very self-conscious history at every pore. She insisted that I would be interested in looking at something there, and as she carefully refused to specify what it was I couldn't really insist that I wouldn't. Her suggestion didn't quite carry the force of a command, but I felt that I wasn't really left with much option. She led me away as soon as she considered that I'd had a decent time to rest my legs after the walk back from the ship (which had, of course, been attended by the blond youth.)

I was surprised to find that the west wing wasn't dressed up, either for use or for tourists. I supposed they didn't get many tourists. Nobody lived in the west wing, but then, nobody lived in a lot of the rooms in the rest of the house either, and they were kept clean and tidy. It would undoubtedly have been wasted effort to maintain the wing in a state of perpetual readiness and tidiness, but in the absence of any kind of servant problem it surprised me that the Wildebloods would allow a substantial part of their mansion to descend into the early stages of decay. Obviously, when James and his son had built the house originally their ambitions had considerably outstripped their needs, but it seemed that subsequent generations hadn't put in the serious work required to catch up. In the main body of the house and the east wing continuous improvements had been made—including the establishment of electric generators in an outbuilding to supply electricity—but the west wing was still cold and lighted—or rather unlighted, until we arrived—by candles.

There was dirt in abundance, webs spun by predatory insects, and signs of fungal decay in the woodwork.

Alice led me through corridors past sealed-up doors until we came to the southern end of the wing—one extremity of the U-shaped house. There, we found a pair of double doors, which she pushed back with some difficulty. They gave access to a large gallery—very long and also very deep, in that its ceiling was the ceiling of the second story. A wide balcony ran around the room where the floor of the second story might have been, but there was still a great vault of unused space. It lent a strange feeling to the place.

It would have made a very impressive banqueting hall—much more impressive than the dining room the family actually used. But it was filled, instead, by oblong boxes on stilts—glass-topped cases. They loomed in the semi-darkness like ranked sarcophagi.

"We'll have to light the candles," said Alice. "Would you . . . ?" She offered me a taper, which I lighted from the candle she was carrying, and went over to the far side of the room. There were twenty brackets, each containing four candles, spaced along the length of the wall. I moved slowly along, lighting each and every one, while Alice did likewise on the other side. It took quite a long time.

Even eighty candles didn't fill the room with brilliance. Their light was yellow but they made everything in the gallery grey . . . grey with dust, with the languid evenness of the long-forgotten. It would have been much easier to see by day, but I had to admit that it had a special kind of impressiveness by night—the black vault above my head, shadowed by the balcony, seemed to hang like a predatory creature over the grimed display cases.

Last night the cemetery, I thought, today the museum. What's left for tomorrow?"

Alice was smiling as she took back the taper and blew it out. It was an attractive smile and, in all likelihood, perfectly sincere. But my attitude to it was the attitude of a wise and ancient fish to a cunningly-wrought fly on an angler's hook. I wasn't biting. She wasn't a beautiful girl—a little too heavily built, although not exactly fat, with hair that was too coarse in texture, very dark brown but not quite black. But her manner was pleasant. There was no trace of Zarnecki's muffled hostility or Philip's lizard-like remoteness.

She gestured with her arm toward the nearest of the cases.

"We don't use this now," she said. "It was great-grandfather's collection. Actually, I mean great-great-great-great-grandfather's, but for convenience ... you know who I mean."

I knew all right. I already knew all about James Wildeblood's sense of the past. I'd never given it a thought in the past, but it seemed obvious to me now. Of course he'd have a museum—an assembly of relics. A collection to display his knowledge of the *flora* and *fauna* of Wildeblood—*his* world. All classified, all labelled. A labor of ... not precisely love ... something more than that, and perhaps, in a way, something less. This was just another facet—but perhaps a significant facet—of his legacy. The legacy of Wildeblood the naturalist.

I went to the nearest case and looked in, half-expecting what I saw.

It was full of seashells.

Row upon row, arranged as per species, genus, family. All named in Latin and numerically coded. All done without the aid of a computer—in fact, probably not on a statistical unit-character comparison at all, but by eye and instinct, the classical way. Wildeblood and Linnaeus both.

They sat upon a sheet of milky glass, black lines

59

painted to link them up in groups. Some of the black lines were dotted, tentative. No one had ever confirmed them. No one had ever bothered to try. This was the work of one man . . . perhaps aided by his children. But this was one legacy he hadn't managed to make meaningful. It endured, but it was dead. Finished, but not complete. A thing like this could never be complete; it had to keep growing, changing, maturing. Here was only the beginning, a bare skeleton of a whole Natural History.

Perversely, I felt almost glad when I looked at it. Glad that somewhere, in something, James Wildeblood had failed.

I moved on to the next case. The dim candlelight sent ripples of light across the uneven glass surfaces as I moved. On a colony world, in its early days, I thought, glass is precious. As precious as iron. How many windows are there in this mansion? How many panes deck these cases? But the equitable division of the colony's wealth had never been the rule here. Quite the reverse, in fact. I removed some of the dirt with my sleeve, to see more clearly what was within.

More shells—calcined relics of the sea's vast population. Everything dry, cold, hard. Nothing to decay. And everything labelled, ranked, linked.

Where did he find the time? I wondered. To *be* everything and to *do* everything. Did he ever sleep? Or is that the real prerogative of a monarch—to be forever doing whatever takes the royal whim. If James Wildeblood couldn't take his hobbies seriously, who could? I wondered about Wildeblood in his twenties and thirties, on Earth . . . a life on a planet squeezed of natural resources, where great wealth had almost ceased to matter in many areas because there was so little it could buy. On Earth, nations owned collections like this. Nations and universities. Not people. How frustrated must Wildeblood have been? How cramped for space to expand and impose his personality upon his environment? He must, I thought, have been a man of truly awesome *greed*, not in terms of piling up credit but in terms of wanting things to belong to him—the kind of things that didn't belong to *any*one on Earth, but to everyone or no one.

"I thought you'd like to see it," said Alice.

"Yes," I said. "It's fascinating."

"You . . . like this kind of thing."

"Yes," I said, though it wasn't really a question.

"You're like . . . him . . . in some ways."

I looked at her sharply, then. She wasn't kidding. It was the work of her imagination, of course, but it was more than just the fact that my job was similar to his. She had an image of James Wildeblood . . . an almost worshipful regard. He'd been half-deified. The things that were known about him, his talents, his interests, had been invested with a certain sacredness. And he was remembered as something slightly alien . . . different.

And here were we . . . outworlders. Strange, different . . . with eccentric interests. Including me. To them I must seem remote, uncommunicative, strange. Unlike Nathan, I didn't try hard to please, I couldn't fit myself into their way of life, their customs, their habits. And I was a biologist. I paid a great deal of attention to things no one else looked at or even noticed. Living things, or the relics of living things.

Was it so surprising that they—some of them, at least—should try to see a little of Wildeblood in me?

Alice was sincere. It prejudiced her in my favor. She was inclined to look at me now through a haze of illusion and belief that blurred her vision somewhat. I thought immediately that I might make this work for me, and—perhaps oddly—I felt a slight twinge of conscience at taking such a coldly pragmatic view.

"I'd like to come here again," I said. "In the daytime. Look at it closely. I'd very much like to get to know your world the way . . . he . . . knew it." I couldn't help the emphasis and the coy hesitation in pronouncing the pronoun. That kind of thing is infectious.

"Yes," she said. "But . . . don't mention it to Philip."

I was taken quite by surprise. "Why not?" I asked.

"He . . . might not like you to come out here."

It occurred to me then that being somewhat reminiscent of James Wildeblood needn't work exclusively to my advantage. Alice might like me for it—but not Philip. And certainly not Zarnecki. They were suspicious of me. To them, the intellectual kinship would make me seem even more of a threat.

"I would have shown you this place earlier," she said. "But there seems to be so little time. You ride out with Elkanah to look at the crops, the people in their homes, the fishermen and their catches, the marketplaces."

"We're only here for a short time," I said. We'd been very careful not to mention how short "short" might be. "There's a great deal we need to know. There's a great deal we might learn from you that might aid other colonies going out to other worlds. In fact, the example of your success might be important in making sure that new colonies *do* go out again, to new worlds. We have to know what problems you've found and how you've overcome them. We need to know how much you've achieved and what you're likely to achieve in the future—the directions in which you're developing. We need to know . . . *everything*."

Now it was me that was trying to be the angler, casting flies on the surface of the pool.

But the fish weren't rising.

"I'm sure that you know everything you need to know," she said. "There's really nothing very complicated about the way we live."

"It's not just a matter of recording endless details," I said. "There are good reasons. You're bound to face problems in adapting to an alien world—problems that might be slow to develop, problems you may not even notice. Some of the crops you brought from Earth haven't taken too well to the soil here. We can try to find out why. Some of the local species of plant and animal appear to have been wiped out, and others are threatened. We can try and work out the ecological consequences. We need to know what effects you've had on the population of the sea in the last hundred years so that we might anticipate any permanent changes you're causing or any problems that may develop in the long term. Your very survival here may depend on what we find . . . I don't say that it will, but it could. You can't afford overconfidence. Not after six generations . . . not after sixty. We're here to help you. Suppose, for instance, that the drug most of the people seem to take was having a serious effect on health . . . effects that you don't correlate with it, or don't even notice because so many people show them that they're accepted as normal. It's in areas like that that you need our help."

She didn't show any overt surprise that I mentioned the drug. Perhaps she assumed that we'd been told, or that I'd simply come across it in the natural course of my investigations. But I wasn't going to persuade her to let go any extra information. She just didn't want to talk about it.

She moved away to another display case, and showed her disinterest in what I'd been saying by taking an undue and entirely false interest in its contents.

"They're very pretty," she said.

These were the products of coralline organisms—dendritic structures and tubes. There were also teguments and spicules from organisms that seemed to fill ecological niches appropriate to Earthly echinoderms but which were put together on different geometrical principles. They weren't very pretty—not even as pretty as the faded shells in the first two cases.

I didn't know whether to press on or not. I decided to soft-pedal. I was, in any case, slightly uncomfortable with Alice. I was apprehensive of the unpredictable.

"It's a pity this place has been neglected," I said. "There's a lot to be learned from it. Don't you teach the colony's children about their world?"

She seemed moderately surprised. "They're taught what they need to know," she said. "How to do what has to be done."

Most of the children received no schooling at all. They were taught to read and write in community classes . . . but the bulk of their education was purely practical. They learned work. Not knowledge for its own sake. Even the aristocracy, it seemed, didn't go in for natural history. What then? I wondered. Not Latin and Greek. Nor scientific theory. Technology, perhaps . . . and the most important thing of all. How to use and manage the heritage of Earth. The library of tapes and microfilms. Some of that was held and used in the colleges. Some had been stored—put away for a few decades or centuries until it might come in handy. The sorting out had, of course, been done by

James Wildeblood, and in all likelihood no one would have seen any reason for rethinking.

"Do you come here often?" I asked, sarcastically, letting my tongue run away with my thoughts momentarily.

She took it, inevitably, at face value.

"Sometimes," she said. "It's a good place to come to be alone."

I judged that "sometimes" wasn't very often. But it wasn't a lie. I looked at the floor, and saw the marks which showed that the dust was, occasionally, disturbed. Countless footprints—impressions going back many years.

I noticed something else, too, as I looked round. Pinned to the wall, near the double door through which we'd entered, was a skin mounted on a panel. The skin looked like plastic—black with a faint dappling of brown and green. . . .

"What's that?" I asked, pointing.

"The skin of a salaman," she said. "It's a very good one. You don't often see them whole, like that—they shed them, you know—sometimes the ones that live on land go back to the sea, and they . . . walk out of their skins. But usually the skins shred and break."

I nodded. For a moment or two, I thought that James Wildeblood might have shot it. A hunting trophy. But that wasn't one of his vices. Not ever.

"It's against the law to kill them, isn't it?" I murmured.

"It's against the law to interfere with them at all," she said. "Nobody does."

At least, I thought, he did that much. He limited his empire to human beings. He didn't try to enslave them, or even to communicate with them.

"Some of our people are trying to make contact with them," I said. "To learn their language. It would be a wonderful thing, if we could do it."

"Why?" she asked. Again, it was sincere and honest. She didn't see why. To her, to all her family, the salamen meant no more than the museum. Forgotten, ignored, unimportant. I wondered, briefly, whether James Wildeblood's dynasty was working out quite the way he'd intended. Had he anticipated such a withdrawal; such a social introversion? Hadn't he expected more?

"Because they're the product of a separate creation," I said. "They're evidence—proof—that the universe contains a potentially infinite number of habitable worlds, intelligent beings. For now, they're one of a handful of representatives of that infinite possibility. Ambassadors, in a sense. If we can talk to them . . . if we can establish some kind of meaningful relationship with them . . . don't you see what kind of a beginning that might be? Don't you see that it takes the human race into an entirely new phase in its existence, its life within the universe?"

She didn't. It didn't matter a damn to her. But who could blame her? She was involved in a different kind of beginning—a kind of recapitulation, a repetition of what man had already gone through on Earth. It was a time of narrow horizons, limited objectives. But it was necessary. Vitally necessary.

"We're very different," I said. "Outworlders and colonists. People of Earth and . . . Wildeblood's people. But there's no reason for mistrust . . . no reason for hatred. You do see that, don't you?"

She stared back into my eyes, still a long way from genuine understanding. We were on different wavelengths, out of tune.

"I'm tired," I said, when she didn't answer. "I think I'd better look at this properly another time."

Without any more ado, we began blowing out the candles.

7

Next day I went back to the *Daedalus* to continue my analysis of the sample that the newsvendor-cum-minstrel had given to me. I checked the treated tissue cultures I'd left overnight and made careful measurements of all the effects. There were no surprises. The most noticeable effect was on nervous tissue, although the whole integrated metabolism was slightly altered.

I spent the greater part of the morning plotting the data and organizing it in order to feed it into the mathematical analogue of functioning brain tissue that we had on the computer. This would give some idea of the likely psychological effects of the drug, although any conclusions drawn would be highly tentative. Even the best simulations still fall a long way short of the real thing. No one's built a person inside a computer yet, or written a program for accurately predicting what people will do or how they'll react to even the simplest chemical stimuli in any real detail. But even fake experiments can sometimes tell you things that you need to know. And I wasn't going to try the stuff out on anyone real until I'd got all the possible data at my fingertips.

By the time it got to the midday meal I had just about everything on paper that I was going to get, and it was time to move on to stage three.

Without much optimism, I called for volunteers.

Only Pete and Karen were there—Nathan was away with Miranda yet again.

"You want me to act as a guinea pig?" asked Pete.

"I've just enough left for one good hype," I said. "Pity to waste it."

"No," he said shortly.

"You have to be joking," said Karen. "And besides which, does tradition count for nothing? You're supposed to be your own guinea pig."

"It's not dangerous," I assured them.

"That's what Daedalus said to Icarus," replied Karen.

"Icarus was an idiot," I informed her. "He didn't read the instructions properly."

"Nevertheless," she said, with an air of finality, "fools rush in while angels practice the better part of valor. You shoot it, I'll watch."

I sighed. "You'd better," I agreed. "If I go berserk someone has to render me unconscious. And if there's anything that I haven't foreseen, you'd better take notes. If I die of it, I'll never forgive you."

It was not, of course, the first time that I'd been required as experimental subject as well as experimenter. The subjective angle is always useful when you're attempting to analyze psychotropic effects. But it was a business I'd always found distasteful, and likely always would. In addition, I still had the memory of an unexpected and completely unprepared encounter with a rather nasty psychotropic on Dendra.

I couldn't help wishing, as I prepared the dose, that Conrad or Linda was around. I wouldn't have been short of a volunteer then.

The locals, not unnaturally, would take the drug orally rather than intravenously. Probably they sprinkled it on food, or dissolved it in warm soup. It would take longer to act that way and the effects would extend over a somewhat longer period. They would probably take a larger dose than I intended to take, though, and I wanted to get the full benefit of mine as soon as possible.

I injected into a vein in my left forearm. That was more or less a matter of habit, because I now used my left hand as much as my right. Ever since I'd been mauled by a panther on Dendra my right arm had been a little stiff, and I found it painful to do any heavy work with that arm.

I retired to my cabin to lie on the bed. I took a tape recorder and switched it on so that I could record anything that I might not remember later on. Karen came too, as a safeguard against anything unexpected.

For the first couple of minutes there was no sound except the faint whirr of the tape spool.

Then Karen got impatient. "Can I talk?" she asked, in a half-whisper.

"Might as well," I said. "No use pretending we're in a hospital drama."

"Not that I've got anything to say," she added. "But I thought I'd better check."

"Have you cracked that code yet?" I asked.

"In a word," she replied, "no. Have you?"

"No time," I said. "Spent last night in the museum. Haven't had a free moment."

"Try now," she suggested. "You might get a blinding flash of inspiration while you're high. Better than seeing hallucinations or imagining that you're chatting with God."

I took off my wristwatch and held it up in front of my face, letting my head relax against the pillow.

"It's taking effect pretty quickly," I said—talking for the tape recorder rather than for Karen. "It's going to my head. Slight feeling of giddiness. I'm not used to it, though. It feels strange. No nausea. I can feel my heartbeat—and the pulse at the side of my head. But the tick of the watch isn't any louder, nor is the sound of my voice. Clenching my fist feels . . . odd. It's not an exaggeration of the sensations . . . just an awareness in the brain. I feel . . . more alive. I can see perfectly, but the image looks . . . not *flat*, exactly, but . . . more remote. It's more like an image and less like a reality . . . it doesn't seem so much a part of me, as though the connection is looser. This is something internal . . . a feeling of well-being. It's pleasant. I feel . . . *me*. Larger, I think . . . no, not in size . . . as if I were more *solid*, more *material*. That's it. Not bulk or heaviness . . . just a sense of *completeness*, of *me*-ness. Crazy . . . but it's an odd feeling.

"My hand's steady. My speech isn't blurring, but I'm beginning to feel the same kind of remoteness from the sound that I am from the visual image. It's almost as though I were seeing a picture and hearing a tape. Curious. I don't feel intoxicated. I'm calm, not excited. But I feel as if I shouldn't be lying down. I want to *move*. I can feel my muscles, and I want to use them. I can move my arms, but it's not enough. Clenching my fist . . . tensing my fingers . . . is pleasant. But when I hit my palm with my fingernails it still hurts. I'm not anaesthetized. But there's more *pleasure* in simply being . . . in movement, in *aliveness*. . . ."

I sat up.

"Hold it!" said Karen. "Oh hell, I suppose I should have got this straightened out beforehand. What am I supposed to do, restrain you?"

I could feel myself smiling.

"It isn't instant schizophrenia," I said. "In all likelihood the locals spend half their lives hopped up on this stuff. It doesn't stop them getting on with life . . . quite the reverse, in fact. I'm going outside. Bring the recorder."

"I don't know that it's a good idea," she said. "And standing orders . . ."

70

"Then stay. I'm going."

She stood up as I moved for the door. "I'm still not sure I oughtn't to belt you," she said. "But you know what they say about madmen having the strength of ten, and I guess you may need looking after more than the ship does. . . . Wait a minute!"

I was already on my way. She paused to grab the recorder, and followed.

"Hold the mike up," I told her, when we'd negotiated our way through the airlock and were face to face with the great outdoors.

"I feel energetic," I told it. "Not infused with any superhuman kind of strength, but tuned up . . . in good shape."

I began to walk away, feeling the spring in my step. A hundred and fifty yards away a cottage door opened.

"Bastards," I muttered, and then said: "Come on, let's make the buggers work for their coin for once."

I broke into a loose-limbed jog-trot, heading away from the ship down the slope toward the gully that ran down toward the dunes and the sea.

Karen swore. "If I didn't know that you were always considerably less than sane," she said, raising her voice as I moved away, "I wouldn't give a credit note for your assurances now." But she started running too. Away to our right, in the cottage, there was considerable excitement. This was probably making their day. Action at last!

"The movement is pleasurable," I reported to the microphone, when Karen caught up. "Using the muscles I can feel . . . or imagine that I feel . . . the heat in them . . . the chemistry of the action . . . almost an effervescence . . . a liquid sensation . . . it's good . . . let's go . . ."

I accelerated, not to a sprint but to a comfortable coasting pace, taking long, easy strides.

"This is the last time I help *you* in one of your filthy experiments," said Karen, punctuating it with desperate attempts to pump her lungs more effectively. She was taller than the average, but her stride was inches short of mine. She had to take extra paces. But she still kept up.

I forgot about the tape recorder. It was no longer necessary, let alone convenient.

I ran across fallow fields, along the streamless ribbon of mossy soil in the valley cleft, over the sandy ridge which separated the cultivated land from an expanse of dunes where land was slowly being reclaimed from the sea. The prevailing wind blew from the west, and it was in my face. My feet sank into the soft sand at every step, holding me back, threatening to throw me off balance. I felt exhilarated.

The exhilaration wasn't the primary effect of the drug—it was a secondary effect made possible by the drug's action. Most of my subjective responses were secondary effects, no doubt connected with the fact that this was my first encounter with it. People who used it regularly, were accustomed and addicted to it, would have different subjective responses. But what was *basic* to the whole experience, intrinsic, was the feeling of involvement with my physical being, the sensation of wholeness. I was self-confined, but also self-*filling*. I felt that I had a far clearer notion of myself as opposed to the universe which contained me, surrounded me and invaded me through my senses.

The grass which bound the dunes, spiky and stiff, crackled beneath my feet. The dunes became looser and more undulating as we got nearer to the sea. Running up an especially steep one because I couldn't be bothered to go round it I found my feet battling for hopeless purchase in soft sand that gave way and spilled me back in a miniature landslide. I fell forward on to the face of the dune, letting my hands drive into the sand. It felt suddenly still and peaceful, because we were in the lee of the dune and the sharp salt wind was gone.

I turned over and relaxed, my breath coming in great gasps as my body fought to pay off the oxygen debt incurred by the muscles. I could almost feel the lactic acid cycle whirring away like some dynamic factory process in an automated plant.

Karen sank to her knees in the drift of loose sand I'd spilled from the dune.

"The least you could have done," she panted, "was give me a dose too. Some pep pill!"

"I offered," I said. "Never say I didn't offer. Guaranteed to turn a ten stone intellectual into an Olympic champion. . . ."

"I, too, could have a body like yours, hey?"

"Quite so," I said. "So be careful."

I felt waves of relaxation oozing through me while my limbs recovered, returning to metabolic ground state. The languor was delightful . . . but by no means delirious. I was still thinking clearly, still in control. I noticed that the spool was still going round.

"It's okay," I said to the mike. "Results in. As expected. Confirm hypothesis."

"The natives are all on this stuff permanently?" asked Karen.

"I'd bet on it," I said. "Maybe even Philip himself, though that's less obvious. It's good stuff. Wildeblood must have discovered it, analyzed it, maybe even tried it out in the course of his routine experiments. To anyone else, it might have been interesting, maybe even significant. It has medical possibilities, though its synthesis from raw materials available on Earth would probably be incredibly expensive. If, in the far, far future there's ever such a thing as interstellar trade, this stuff is worth money. But to Wildeblood, the medical possibilities weren't even in the race. He saw others. And now we have a colony of addicts."

"How addictive is it?" she asked.

"Fearsomely," I told her. "Withdrawal would be extremely unpleasant . . . it wouldn't kill, but this is one of those things where the disease is emphatically to be preferred to the cure."

"Could you help to break it gently?" she said.

"Sure," I told her. "I could treat the symptoms, get people through the withdrawal syndrome without too much hassle . . . no worse than a heavy cold. But where's the demand? You have to remember that people *like* the damn thing. It's good stuff. Offer a man a choice between a relatively easy way to break the habit and an assured supply for life and he'll go for the second every time. What do the side effects matter to him, especially if he's been on the stuff all his life?"

"What are the side-effects?"

"Shorter life-expectancy—the body wears out earlier. There's no ripe old age on Wildeblood. Then there's the damping of aggressiveness, lowering of intelligence. They're not direct effects of the drug but they're encouraged by it and are inevitable corollaries of long-term usage and physiological dependence. Another effect is lowering resistance to disease. That isn't much of a problem here—yet. The original colonists were debugged as thoroughly as possible, and the infectious diseases they brought with them are relatively mild. At the same time, no micro-organisms in the local life-system have yet contrived an adaptive mutation which will make humans good hosts. The re-emergence of serious disease is a crisis just about all the colonies will face in time, and it will be deadly serious for all of them. This colony will have a problem of slightly greater magnitude than most. If the situation is touch and go, this colony will go where another one might have touched.

"That's bad, in its own way. But there are other, more subtle things . . . maybe insidious, if you're of the mind to call them names. Because the drug is *good*, because it works, it breeds contentment. It breeds lack of ambition. All relative, of course, relative to Earth. It made the early generations amenable to Wildeblood rule, amenable to filling their allotted places in the fight to make the colony viable, establish its self-supporting systems. But it's making the later generations—the *now* generations—satisfied with what they have. It's not encouraging new drive, new ambition . . . and is probably inhibiting them. Wildeblood's scheme has worked beautifully, but there's still nothing *outside* that original scheme, and there may never be.

"Now maybe that's not bad. People tend to react in horror at the idea of a more docile human race, less aggressive, less ambitious . . . ready to settle for what they've got if they can possibly reckon it as enough. But maybe that horror is a bit less than justified. Maybe if things go a little slower, a little more carefully, they have a better chance of ending up where the people really want to go. I'm not sure. I can't say. But those are the things that can be put down as effects of the drug."

"What does it actually do?" she wanted to know. "In crude and simple terms."

"Oh, that . . ." I shrugged, as if it wasn't important, though of course it was—perhaps the most important thing of all. "It's really very simple. It selectively stimulates a certain area of the hind brain, the area that's connected with pleasurable sensations. What it does is to make internal nervous sensations—*not* the reception of sensory stimuli—more pleasurable. So that *using* your body—physical action and manual labor—becomes more pleasurable,

75

and so does the range of sensations by which you actually feel your body . . . *in*voluntary muscular actions like heartbeat. You see why it militates against purely cerebral activity? Why it breeds contentment with what we might consider a hard and unrewarding lot?"

"So why is hard labor still a punishment in the legal set-up?" she asked.

"It's not the labor itself," I pointed out. "It's the conditions of labor. Not the doing itself but the where and the when and the how . . . see?"

She nodded.

"And so," I said. "We leave them to it. We let them get on with it. They've made their bed, as the saying goes, and it's not for us to tip them out of it. Nor is it for us to interfere with the politics of supply. My good friend Cyrano de Bergerac can whistle for his secrets, which I haven't found out in any case. It's all very clear and straightforward."

"But . . . ?" she prompted.

"What but?" I countered.

"Come on, Alex," she said. "I *know* you. I never heard you make a speech yet without a 'but' in it. When you say that it's all straightforward you mean that it's all straightforward *but*. So . . . but what?"

"Well," I confessed, "there is one thing that worries me."

"Which is?"

"Nathan. In his eyes, this colony is a resounding success. I don't suppose he likes Philip and his regime any better than I do. But Nathan's a practical man. He'll put up with it. And if that's the price for a successful colony, that's the price he's willing to recommend to the UN. But if Nathan does go back to the UN to say 'It can be done. It has been done. It can be done again . . .' and holds up this colony as his glowing example, he's putting forward a prospectus for colonies with all the inbuilt vulnerabilities I talked about. Well, that's as may be, *but*, and here it is, where does that leave me? If I say 'No. This is not the way to mount successful colonies—it's highly dangerous and suspect, and may lead to disaster' I may be throwing away one of the best advertisements we have for the reinstitution of the colony program. It's the double bind all over again. If I tell the truth—the whole, unblemished truth—I may subvert my own ends.

"*I* believe—devoutly—that despite all these difficulties, all these dangers, all these exceptions and questions and problems, we must continue—or begin again—to send colonies into space. But it isn't a matter of belief. It's a matter of convincing the UN that it's a politically viable and defensible move to do so. And as Nathan perpetually points out, to achieve that end politically we have to advertise, we have to make our arguments strong and beautiful. We *can't* go back to Pietrasante and say: 'Every colony is facing the possibility of disaster, and even the ones which have done well are still in trouble and are not examples to be copied.' That would be instant death. We need to say: 'Here are colonies surviving, and we have found the keys to their survival. As a result of what we have learned we can now promise that future colonies will have every chance of success.' It may be a lie, but it's a necessary lie.

"The trouble is—if I collaborate in concocting an advertising fiction to sell the idea of colonization back to the UN, I become a party not just to selling the idea but also to selling the fiction. And that I don't like. Not only because of the principle involved but because the fiction itself may be dangerous and none too palatable. See?"

She saw. She'd seen it building up over the

course of the mission. Maybe she'd even seen, right back at the beginning, that it was inevitable.

"You spend too much time wrestling with your conscience, Alex," she said. "Either be cynical or be stupid, but make up your mind. You've only two choices. Play it Nathan's way or say goodbye—at least for another hundred and fifty years—to extrasolar expansion. For all the hoping you do and all the intellectual doublethinking there *isn't* another way, and there won't be."

I was going to thank her, with all due bitterness. But I only got to open my mouth before we were interrupted. A silhouette appeared on top of the dune. It was Nathan. He was looking all around, staring across the expanse of undulating sand and spiky grass. He was looking for something. Us.

"We're down here," I said. I couldn't help the fact that the remark was drenched with the acid that I'd been holding for what I'd intended to say.

But he didn't notice. He was slightly ruffled— which, for a man of Nathan's temperament, signalled extreme dismay.

"Back to the ship," he said. "Quickly. There's trouble."

We came to our feet immediately. "What kind of trouble?" I asked.

Now it was he that sounded bitter. "Calm down," he said. "We're not under attack. Yet. No need for action stations. But events are under way ... we have to talk."

"About what?" I asked.

We were already walking back in the direction of the *Daedalus*. I looked round, trying to spot our cohort of shadows. But they were out of sight, for once. The dunes gave ample opportunity for discretion.

"About a diplomatic incident," he said. "Which,

it will no doubt make your day to hear, *I* have pro-voked. Single-handedly. Foolishly."

His tone was so drastic in its self-condemnation that I almost felt disposed to sympathy. I didn't, at any rate, feel amused. I wasn't about to get sarcas-tic, either.

"What did you do?" I asked.

"I was set up," he replied. "Zarnecki wants to fight me. With swords. Tomorrow noon."

It took a moment to catch on.

"Are you trying to say that you've been chal-lenged to a *duel*?" said Karen, unbelieving.

I could almost sense the way he gritted his teeth as he said: "Yes."

8

By the time we got back to the ship I was feeling sober. The drug was still working its magic in my brain but I was using my strength of mind against it now. I clamped down on the urge to be moving, to be active, to be *using* all the muscles I had just got to know properly for the first time. It wasn't too hard to do. I still had clarity of thought and strength of purpose.

We assembled for conference—all four of us.

"How did you manage to get yourself challenged to a duel?" demanded Karen. I could tell from the way she phrased the question that the opportunity to score a few cutting sentences off Nathan wasn't going completely to waste, but even Karen was prepared to take things easier. She could have been even nastier.

"Do you want to hear the pretext or do you want me to speculate about the reason?" he snapped back.

"Both," I said, in a calming voice. "Start with the one and work your way into the other."

"The pretext," he said, levelly, "was that I besmirched the honor of the family by seducing Miranda."

"And did you?" asked Karen.

Nathan hesitated. Karen raised her eyes as if in appeal to heaven. Nathan's displeasure was intensified.

"It wasn't like that!" he said—not the kind of thing one would normally expect to find tumbling from his thin lips.

"Don't tell me," said Karen. "It was love at first sight, right?"

"Had I known that it was a set up," said Nathan, somehow recapturing his temper, "I would have been aware that my actions were . . . undiplomatic. However, I did not know. And because I took the circumstances . . . perhaps naively . . . at face value, it seemed to me that to act otherwise might have been . . . equally undiplomatic."

"You pays your money and you takes your chance," I muttered. And added, silently: What price lust at first sight?

"All right," said Pete, trying to smooth things out. "Let's not bother with the details. What are they trying to achieve? Presumably it *isn't* just a private grudge on Zarnecki's part?"

"It might be," said Nathan, "but no serious student of probability would bet on it. It was arranged. Staged."

"Why?" I asked.

"They're trying to put pressure on us. It's called letting us know we aren't wanted here. On top, they're smooth and nice and they've vacuumed the welcome mat. And Philip's position isn't prejudiced—outwardly, it's nothing to do with him and he doesn't know about it. Underneath, they want us to leave. They want to embarrass us. They want us to rush through whatever we came to do and then go home—without there being any long-term consequences with regard to Earth. They think they're pretty clever. If we back out after this, it looks like our fault. Philip keeps his image as a benevolent father-figure. You can see the pattern—and the thinking behind it."

"And when we don't take the hint?"

Nathan shrugged. "I assume that tomorrow is just for show. Zarnecki will give me a scar—a warning. He isn't disposed to homicide. But we all know what happens to people who don't take hints. They get hinted at harder. People can get hurt, you know. *Accidents*, I believe, is the correct euphemism. Then again, maybe we could be attacked by dissidents or rebels—so that a very surprised and injured Philip can make profuse apologies and tell us that it shows how necessary law and order is."

"You make it sound like gangsterism," said Karen.

"The politics of intimidation," he corrected her. "It's only gangsterism when criminals do it."

"So what do we do?" asked Pete. "Pull out?"

"Maybe," said Nathan. "It could be the best course. On the other hand, there may be room for a little haggling yet. Zarnecki wants something from us before we go, if you remember."

"The code," I said.

"Precisely. So the situation is a little more complicated than simply wanting us gone. They'd like us out of the way . . . but they'd also like to use us, if they can. And while they're trying to play it both ways, we have a breathing space."

"Now wait just a minute," I said. "All this is fine—but it's also very speculative. You may see potential for doing a little double-dealing, but for the moment I can see potential for your getting yourself killed. How can you be sure Zarnecki only intends to put on a demonstration tomorrow?"

"He's not just a killer," said Nathan. "And to him, a duel isn't just an excuse for a quick burst of violence. To you, it may seem like a joke, but here duelling is meaningful."

"It's still the twenty-fourth century here," said Karen. "Even if the technology looks more like the nineteenth."

"That's not the point," said Nathan. "Technology has nothing to do with it. Duelling is a social institution linked to certain sociopolitical circumstances. On Earth, societies are integrated to the extent that the state takes over all the responsibilities of protecting the individual and his property. In case of assault or theft the police and the courts are the only legal channel of recrimination. But that's only possible where there's a high degree of social organization, whether the government is autocratic or democratic. Here, we have a population much more widely dispersed, with individual communities much less highly organized. Despite the elementary divisions of labor here villages and families are still in large measure divorced and independent from the support of the whole social organism. There's a police force and there are courts, but to a large extent the responsibility for the protection of the individual, his family and his property rests with him.

"In barbaric societies the principal instrument of restitution and revenge is the blood-feud. In societies more civilized that becomes ritualized and less deadly—it becomes a system of personal honor, where questions are settled by a contest whose outcome is final. The escalation of the blood-feud, with whole families being entangled in bloody conflicts down the generations, is subverted. What's more, in a situation where a small aristocracy defined by family ties rules over a large commonalty, the duelling system may become a useful tool in social control. If duelling is accepted among the aristocracy as a means of settling disputes while disputes in the lower classes are supposedly to be settled by the courts, members of the aristocracy not being expected to demean themselves by fighting with those beneath them, then effectively the lower classes have no means of redress *at all* with respect to injuries sustained at the hands of aristocracy. In a situation such as we have in this colony ... duelling means something. It's very important."

"What you're trying to get at," I said, "is that from Zarnecki's viewpoint, the duel has to go by the book. He isn't just starting a fight; he's going through a ritual, making a point formally."

"That's right," said Nathan. "And what the book says is that he'll wound me. Just enough to draw blood. It's illegal here to kill anyone in a duel or even to incapacitate them permanently. Colonies can't be wasteful of manpower. Duels to the death only take place in cases of extreme grievance."

"Where'd you get all this fascinating information about local customs?" asked Karen.

"Where'd you think?" he shot back. There was no mistaking the tone of the answer. He'd got it from Miranda—where else? Zarnecki had challenged him, Miranda had made certain he knew exactly where he stood. All part of the game.

"Do you know anything about fencing?" I asked.

"Fencing, no," he said. "But handling a sword ... just a little."

"Is there a difference?" asked Pete.

"Believe it or not," said Nathan, "I once contemplated a career in acting. I trained as an actor, for a while. Classical. I had lessons in stage fighting. Not fencing—just pretend fencing. I know the moves and I can look good. But I don't know anything about genuine attack—just mock attack and how to counter mock attacks."

I couldn't quite suppress the laugh that rose in response to a sudden silly thought.

"What's that for?" he asked.

"Cyrano de Bergerac," I murmured. Then I shook my head and said: "Nothing. Just a thought."

"At least you'll be able to lose gracefully," put in Karen.

I remembered why I had asked about fencing in

the first place. "Let's not rush things," I said. "He hasn't lost yet."

"Don't mind him," said Karen, to Nathan. "He's high on the local pep pills. Thinks he can lick anyone."

I ignored her. To Nathan, I said: "You reckon that this duel really means something to Zarnecki?"

He nodded.

"Supose you were to win it?" I asked.

He was willing to take it seriously, at least as a hypothesis. He considered it for a few moments. "It would make things complicated," he said. "They'd find it very disconcerting. It might put them in something of a quandary—and give us more room for negotiation, as well as more time. What makes you think I might win?"

"Because of what Karen says," I told him. "This afternoon I've been high on a drug the colonists use. It *does* make you feel as if you could lick anyone. It stimulates the nervous tissue in the brain involved with pleasurable sensation. Even actions controlled by the autonomic nervous system become hooked up into the pleasure syndrome—but in order to hook them up there has to be a slowing down of the reflexes. And . . ."

"And Zarnecki is probably on the drug?" Nathan finished for me.

"An addict," I confirmed.

"So I'll have the edge as regards speed . . . but even so. . . ."

"You can have twice the edge if you want it," I said. "He's doped to go slow. . . . I can dope you with something that has the opposite effect . . . speed you up. Zarnecki may be good, by local standards—but it's likely he's never before faced an opponent not on the local drug, let alone one who's *really* juiced up. It's no racing certainty, but it gives you a chance. . . ."

85

"It might at that," said Nathan. "It might at that."

I felt slight misgivings. There was no telling what winning a duel might do to his already colossal ego. He fancied himself quite enough as it was.

He stood up, looking a great deal happier than he had when he'd sat down.

"I'm going back to the house," he said.

"The house!" said Karen, in a tone so replete with astonishment that it was almost comic. "Are you crazy?"

"Not at all," he said. "It's the only thing to do. Treat the duel as duels are meant to be treated—private affairs quite outside the normal course of social affairs. I shall go back to the house as if nothing had happened. Philip and Zarnecki will conduct themselves in the same manner. It might open up certain new possibilities for ironic undertones in the conversation, but that's all. Coming, Alex?"

I shook my head.

"You can have the ironic undertones to yourself," I said. "I don't have your talent for innuendo. I've got to clear up the lab after all the messing about with the drug, and finish up recording the results of the experiment. It'll take a while. I'll walk back later, although you can ask Elkanah to drive out with a carriage to pick me up if it starts to rain. No point in getting wet, is there?"

He smiled, and nodded. "I'll do that," he said. He really was in a better mood. Now I'd offered him a chance I think he was actually looking forward to the prospect of an affair of honor. Maybe it wouldn't take him long to begin congratulating himself for cunningly trapping Zarnecki into challenging him.

"Nathan," I called, as he went out.

He looked back, questioningly.

"You could thank me," I suggested.

"Sure," he said, raising a hand in a kind of salute. "Thanks."

Always the diplomat, I thought, you sycophantic bastard.

And having mentally scored one to myself, I got up and went to the lab, to tidy up after the long investigation.

9

It did start to rain, and they did send Elkanah out with a carriage. Not being able to tell a landau from a surrey with a fringe on top I have no idea how to identify it in one word, but it had only one horse, two wheels and a big leather canopy to keep the rain off.

He'd been waiting quite some time for me—it was dark now—but he made no complaint as I hauled myself up to sit beside him.

"Sorry to keep you," I said, with a cheerfulness that was desperately overdone. "Hope you didn't get cold. You could have sheltered in the cottage over there, of course . . . always people popping in and out of it."

He didn't say anything, but maintained what I took to be his version of a respectful silence. He flipped the rump of the horse with the tip of a long, thin whip, and then steered it round to head downhill toward the road. There was a lantern secured to the edge of the canopy on his side, and it swung lazily from side to side with the motion of the horse, squeaking slightly.

The road was a rutted track which had quickly become something of a morass thanks to the rain. The wheels made a peculiar liquid noise as they whirled through the wood, rather like someone drinking noisily. Any pedestrians we might have passed would have been well and truly spattered. But there seemed to be no one on the road. I sometimes wondered whether it was simply a little-used road or whether the word had gone out that it was to be avoided if humanly possible for the duration of our visit.

We went over and around a couple of low hills, and then came to a moderately-extensive patch of woodland which masked, on the one side, the land marked out for the cemetery, while on the other it stretched away to become rather desolate scrubland as it slowly invaded the dunes.

He had to slow down because with the sky full of rainclouds it was pitch dark except for our lantern, which was by no means in the best place to illuminate our way. The road ran fairly straight and the horse might be assumed to know its way pretty well, but it was definitely no place for reckless driving.

I was content to sit back in my seat, restfully enjoying the ride, and I was almost closing my eyes when there was a sudden flurry of movement. I couldn't see a thing but there was a terrible lurch as the horse stopped and someone or something hurled itself at the carriage from the far side, mounting the running-board forward of the wheel.

Elkanah barely got out a gasp, that might have been a yell if it hadn't been strangled. He was jerked forward from his position and by the light of the lantern I caught a glimpse of a rainswept face and an arm which closed on the servant's clothing just below the neck.

As the face swung backwards and the lantern's own swing sent the shadow of the canopy forward Elkanah was dragged into the gloom. I heard him hit the ground and then, within an instant, there was the sound of another heavy blow.

The thought that flashed into my mind was that they'd killed him. And the thought which followed lightning-fast on its heels was the remembrance of something Nathan had said only a couple of hours before.

Accidents, I believe, is the correct euphemism, then again, maybe we could be attacked by dissidents or rebels, so that a very surprised and injured Philip can make profuse apologies. . . .

It seemed that they weren't waiting until after the duel before providing me with a little lesson. . . .

I didn't wait. With a colossal bound I leapt from the floor of the carriage, clearing the tangle of apparatus that bound it to the horse. I landed on my feet, quite blind to what was ahead of me, and set off at a fast sprint in a direction diagonally away from the road. I didn't know where I was going—I just wanted to get away as far and as fast as possible before I was murdered or beaten up.

I heard a muffled curse behind me, and the sound of someone coming after me.

I didn't hear anything else because I was met with a tremendous blow across the forehead. It wasn't a fist or a club—I'd run straight into a low bough. It gave under the impact and bent back, but it was no twig and I'd been moving at quite some speed. I was knocked sick, but not quite senseless. I rocked back on my heels and fell over.

I tried to stand up again, but my head was reeling. I managed to get to one knee, but couldn't lift myself.

A hand fell on my shoulder, gripping hard.

"Keep still you damned fool!" hissed a hoarse voice, which seemed strangely familiar.

I struggled somewhat—more for show than in any realistic endeavor to escape the grip.

"Wait!" he hissed again. Then, to someone else: "Bring that light!"

I looked back, and saw nothing but a colossal looming shadow. But then someone ran up with the lantern. The man who carried it was big and broad—and also completely unknown to me. But the other man—the one who held me—was immediately recognizable by courtesy of a large and pointed nose.

My head was still unsteady. I put my hands up to my temples. There was no blood but there was a large soft bump. It would probably grow into a magnificent bruise.

I looked up at the big man.

"We can't go on meeting like this," I said.

"Can you stand up?" he asked, concerned for my health.

I tried, and found that I could.

"Do I take it that when you said you'd contact me again this is what you meant?" I asked. "Or are you acting in your professional capacity as highwayman?"

"You've had two days," he said. "I thought it was time for a progress report."

"You're in a hell of a hurry," I said. "Is Elkanah dead?"

"No. But his headache is likely to be worse than yours."

I touched the bump again. "I suppose it's just as well I did this," I murmured. "Help to make the whole scene look convincing, won't it."

"I'll have that as well," he said, pointing to my wrist.

I contemplated refusing. Every gram counted when they made up inventories for the *Daedalus*, and I didn't have a spare. It was probably the only watch on Wildeblood apart from the ones my comrades were wearing. Finally, I said: "You can borrow it. But I want it back. It's no use to you— it's too easily recognizable. You'd better take this as well."

This was a flashlight I was carrying in my pocket.

"Anything else?" he asked.

"A bit of paper with numbers written on it," I

told him. "But you wouldn't want to rob me of that, would you?"

He put away the wristwatch and the torch. His dark eyes were gleaming in the lantern-light.

"You know what the key to the code is?"

I shook my head.

"The drug, then?"

"I've analyzed it. I can let you have the chemical formula—not that it'd mean much. I can give you a comprehensive list of its effects. I could even make up something for you that would make breaking the habit a bit easier."

"Do you know where it comes from?" he demanded, his voice harsh and unnaturally high-pitched.

"No," I said.

He looked angry. He looked ready to disbelieve me. He was thinking that he hadn't got much return on his investment. I got the impression I might not get my wristwatch back.

"Look," I said. "It belongs to a class of biochemical compounds that are fairly common in organisms of all kinds here. There's no reference to it in the survey reports. Given time, and a bit of luck, I might find the plant or animal which manufactures it, or—given more time and a little ingenuity—I might be able to find a product similar enough to make it from by some kind of synthetic process that's not too difficult. But I can't do it overnight."

"How much time?" he asked.

I hesitated. I was stalling him. If I found the answer I very likely wouldn't give it to him. I tried to weigh up what kind of an answer he might accept. I had to keep him on a string if possible. He might not be destined to get anything out of me, but there was something more I wanted out of him.

"Three weeks," I said. It was a preposterous answer. Even if I worked flat out trying to identify the source only serendipity could deliver it to me within six months.

But he wasn't over-enamored of the answer as I gave it.

"You think you'll still be around in three weeks?" he asked.

"Oh," I said. "I see the motive for your sense of urgency now. You heard about the duel, and you figured Philip and Zarnecki were beginning to lean on us. That's why you arranged this little charade at short notice."

"I need to know," he said. "You know why. You can see how things are."

I nodded. "I see your problem," I assured him. "But you can see ours. I don't think they suspect that you've contacted us—although they may suspect after tonight's incident. But they still aren't making it easy for us. That's up to *you*. We need more help."

"What kind of help?"

"Anything you can give us. We need to know everything you know. And if you expect us to break the code then you'll have to tell us what you know about that, why you think it bears upon the rest of the problem, and . . . you'll *have* to give us the whole message."

That was a big heap of demands. Effectively, I was asking him to tell us everything and trust us to play straight with him. And we weren't going to. We'd double cross him all the way. I couldn't help feeling guilty. And a little bit ashamed. In his position, what would I be doing? From his point of view he was fighting the good fight. Only we weren't in the market for fights. Civil wars are bad publicity.

I watched his face while he thought about it. I noticed that he didn't look at the man who held the lantern, although the man who held the lantern was watching *him.* I noticed for the first time that there were more of them. There was a man holding the horse, and a shadow beyond the carriage that might have been a fourth. A jolly little band of outlaws. There were no prizes for guessing which one was Robin Hood—big nose regardless.

"If I'm going to trust you," said the big man, "I want you to remember that it was me that gave you the drug. And the code. If it wasn't for me you wouldn't have a chance of finding out what goes on here. And I also want you to remember what happened here tonight. It could happen again. But not for show. I need your help. Right now, you're asking for mine. If I don't get what I need from you, you won't get away. Philip can't protect you."

I was feeling distinctly uneasy, and it wasn't the bump on the head. This man meant what he said. And Philip *couldn't* protect us, even if he wanted to. I was trying to play both ends against the middle, and all I'd got so far was the prospect of being leaned on by both sides.

Discretion is the better part of valor, I thought. What price recalling the expeditionary force and skipping out? It might be a good idea. We could put together some kind of report on the colony....

But I knew we weren't going to run out. We still had to find out what made this colony tick. Even Nathan wasn't the kind of man to back away from someone's dread secret without making every effort to find out what it was.

"The coded message was left by James Wildeblood," said the man with the large nose. "There must be a dozen copies still floating loose in the colony. We don't know what's in it, but we know he didn't leave it floating about for fun. The word is that *nobody* can read it—not even Philip. If anyone but Wildeblood ever knew, the others must

94

have died with the secret. So rumor has it—and it isn't one of my rumors. I believe it. As to what it is . . . we think it's instructions on how to find and isolate the drug. We think it's a kind of legacy—for all the people, and not just the family."

I'd heard of wishful thinking, but that, as he said it, was just too much to swallow. I didn't say anything, but I was sure that he had to be wrong. To me, that didn't sound like James Wildeblood at all. What was he supposed to be—some kind of historical practical joker? Or a man with a deep-seated heart of gold which made him want to die knowing that his carefully-established dynastic autocracy wasn't going to last forever, but that true democracy would one day prevail? No—that wasn't James Wildeblood.

But . . . given that . . . why *had* he left a coded message?

Or was the rumor, too, just a load of moonshine?

"What about the rest of it?" I said, calmly. "We can't crack a code from that tiny fragment. We need the whole thing. Otherwise our computer is useless. We can't do any kind of frequency analysis without much more data. If you want the answer, you have to let us have the problem."

"I'll get it," he said. "Tomorrow night."

"How will you get it to me?"

"You'll have to meet me. Same time as before. Same place."

"The cemetery, after midnight."

"That's right," he growled. "You'll have to get away again. It shouldn't be difficult."

"How about you?" I asked. "Won't this little operation stir up something of a fuss? They may not be looking for you, but they'll be out searching for *someone*."

"I can look after myself," he assured me. He didn't sound worried. I was willing to bet that he could. He turned to the nearest of his compatriots. "Put the lamp back on the hood," he said. Then, to me: "You should be able to bring the servant round. Drive him home and demand to know why you aren't being properly protected."

"Are you sure there's nothing more?" I asked, in a low, serious voice. "Anything at all that could help me."

He began to shake his head, then said: "All I can tell you is that the drug comes from this island. From the house itself, as far as we can tell. If it goes into the house before it comes out we've never been able to see it."

He was in shadow now, as the lantern was carried back to its rightful place. He didn't say goodbye. All three—or maybe four—of them were lost in the trees in a matter of moments.

I fingered the bump on my forehead yet again.

Next time, I promised myself silently, I'll try to look where I'm going.

10

I managed to bring Elkanah round without wasting too much time. He'd been turned over a time or two while they were presumably going through his pockets, and he was pretty comprehensively covered in mud. I was wet, but I'd fallen on grass when the tree had struck me down, and I wasn't particularly dirty.

It had almost stopped raining—there was just a fitful drizzle—but the sky was still overcast. I decided that driving wasn't a good idea. I helped Elkanah, who was dazed and in no fit condition to talk, let alone act, into the carriage, and took down the lantern. Holding it high in my right hand to illuminate the road I took the horse's halter in my left and began to lead it toward the house.

It wasn't far, but with my boots continually being gripped by the glutinous mud and my head throbbing dully I didn't exactly approach the march with a spring in my step. It took time—time for me to get even wetter.

By the time we arrived we were a sorry sight indeed—even the horse looked extremely sad and bedraggled.

We were met at the gate by another servant, who roused the house in a matter of minutes. Commotion took over, and I was hustled indoors to a waiting crowd. It all seemed a bit too much, and I overacted my injury somewhat in order to be allowed to sit down and close my eyes against the dreadfulness of it all.

I wasn't really in a mood to study them closely,

so I have no idea how much suspicion lay underneath all the concern. I told them the bare bones of the story and left them to it, not immediately caring whether they swallowed it utterly or not. But on the surface, at least, they were extraordinarily solicitous. Elkanah was spirited away to be attended in the servant's quarters, but Alice herself applied the warm, damp cloth to my fevered brow.

If anyone knew in his heart of hearts that the whole thing was as genuine as a papier mâché credit card it was Nathan, and he did his best to protect me from cross-examination. He saw to it that I was taken upstairs and put to bed, given a drink and time to rest before they wanted any more detail from me. By that time, I was back in command of my faculties to such an extent that I was ready for the Spanish Inquisition.

Nathan wouldn't allow a crowd, and kept it down to Philip and Zarnecki. It was Zarnecki, naturally enough, who plied the questions. He was the front man. Philip stayed in the background and gave a silent imitation of a man wishing to get the reputation of being eminently sagacious.

"They pulled Elkanah from his seat," I said. "Because of the position of the lantern I couldn't see any of their faces. I jumped down and tried to run away."

Zarnecki looked faintly disgusted by that. On Wildeblood, a man was supposed to stand and fight—weapon or no weapon and no matter what the odds. To hell with that, I thought. I'll plead sanity. It's the only part I can act convincingly.

"You were hit from in front," he pointed out.

"By a tree," I admitted. "I couldn't see where I was running. It got in my way. If it hadn't, they'd never have caught me."

He looked even more disgusted now. It wasn't

the attitude he expected, and it certainly wasn't one he approved of.

"How many of them were there?" he asked.

"I don't know," I replied. "I got the impression of three or four, but I was semi-conscious at best. I didn't actually *see* anything. They took my watch and a flashlight. Maybe there was only one going through my pockets, maybe two. I couldn't tell. I was confused."

He realized that he wasn't going to get much out of me. I presumed that he'd already interviewed Elkanah and got even less. I presumed that I was credible enough.

"We'll get them," said Zarnecki. "If they're on foot they can't get far. We've sent the dogs into the wood with a dozen servants. And the *gendarmes*. At dawn, we'll have another twenty, on horseback. They can't get away, I assure you."

I didn't pass comment. It didn't seem necessary.

"I find it difficult to understand," put in Nathan, "how this happened in the first place. You have us under surveillance twenty-four hours a day, and seem to be sparing no effort in making sure that we're never alone. What good is all that if a thing like this can happen?"

In all probability, they were wondering the same thing themselves.

"You must understand," said Philip, smoothly, "that this kind of incident is not usual. There are thieves on the island, of course, but they do not make a habit of attacking people on the roads in so brutal a fashion. It has never happened in that particular wood, so close to the house."

He stroked his lip thoughtfully. He wasn't a big man—no more than five seven. His head was rounded and the roundness was accentuated by the fact that he kept his hair cropped very short. If he'd had a little less spare flesh he might have been handsome. As it was, his little gestures looked slightly absurd. They didn't do anything for his image at all.

"Perhaps it was our presence here that drew them," I suggested. "It's possible they were under the impression that I would be carrying things which would be very valuable here."

"Yes," said Philip, pensively. "That may be so."

Somehow, I didn't like to see him so thoughtful. Maybe it was just part of the image. Maybe he was suspicious. Or maybe he was thinking that a precedent had been set.

I returned my attention to Nathan and Zarnecki. They were standing a long way apart, not looking at one another. But they weren't being too obvious about it. The duel, for the time being, was shelved. Zarnecki met my eye, and I didn't like the expression on his face. I couldn't evaluate it, but I knew it wasn't friendly. He had taken a dislike to me . . . maybe for no better reason than the fact that I didn't play the formal little games which were so *de rigeur* here, and didn't even try. Perhaps it was more the fact that I didn't even care.

There was a further formal exchange of meaningless phrases, and then Philip and Zarnecki—apparently satisfied that there was nothing further to be done—left us alone.

Nathan sat down on the bed. "What happened?" he asked, in a low voice.

"My friend of the cemetery," I murmured. "Making contact." As I spoke the word "contact" I touched my forehead gingerly.

He smiled.

"And?" he prompted.

"He was persuaded to part with what information he had in hand. The drug is distributed from here, and may be manufactured here. James Wildeblood wrote the coded message. Heaven only knows why—the spiel he gave me was a real farrago. He'll get me the rest tomorrow night. He isn't happy."

"Threats?"

"He did hint that I might run into more trees if we failed to come across with the information he wants. He gives the impression of being a mean man."

"Maybe you should turn him in."

"You sure as hell run a dirty racket," I muttered. "Maybe we should give him what he wants."

"You know we can't do that."

"Speaking personally," I said. "I'm not going to rat on him either. Maybe it's quixotic and downright stupid to leave him loose when I can't deliver the goods, but there are limits."

He didn't give me a lecture on common sense and looking after number one. It wasn't the time or the place. "Have *you* seen any sign of a factory here at the house?" he asked.

I shook my head. "I was over in the west wing last night," I offered, for what it was worth. "Looked dead and dusty to me. But there's a lot of the place we haven't been near. And there's a miscellaneous collection of outbuildings that could be anything. The generators are out there."

He nodded. But his thoughts were somewhere else.

"The thing that puzzles me," I said, "is the raw material. Cyrano de Bergerac and his friends know nothing about it. If it gets in, they don't see it. Or don't recognize it. Could the stuff be refined from something as commonplace as fish or plankton paste? Or is there an acre of deadly weed somewhere in the kitchen garden, pretending to be runner beans?"

He didn't answer. He was hardly listening.

"Something bothering you?" I asked.

"I'm wondering," he said. "I don't know where the hell we're up to in all this. I can't help asking myself whether it's wise to go into that duel tomorrow trying to win. Maybe it would be better in the long run if I just made it look as good as possible and took a dive."

"You better not let him see you do it," I said. "Did you see the look in his eye when I cheerfully admitted to cowardice in the face of the enemy?"

"He's a dangerous man, Alex."

"So are we," I said. "I hope."

"If only they believed us when we tell them we're here to help and have no intention of upsetting their apple-cart. If only they'd just *tell* us how things are."

"Secrets that people are desperately keen to keep," I commented, "are sometimes pretty nasty. Maybe things here are worse than we think."

"Maybe they distil the stuff from human blood," he said, dourly. It was anything but serious, but it led straight on to a thought that *almost* was. I confronted it for a brief instant, then shook my head. "No," I said. "It isn't that."

He nodded agreement.

"You'd better get some sleep," he said. "It's been another long day."

"And tomorrow," I added, "will be even longer."

11

The next day was noticeably warmer, and it seemed as if spring had arrived at last. All the cloud and rain was gone. Nathan and I returned to the ship in the early morning in order to make what preparation we could for the big event. As the weapon to be used in the fight had not been issued to us beforehand Nathan had borrowed a saber of the appropriate size and weight in order to familiarize himself with it and practice a few flourishes. He didn't say exactly where he got it from, but I suspect that one of the younger members of Philip's extended family had helped him out. I expect that Zarnecki was suitably amused.

Owing to the lack of space inside the ship Nathan had to put on his exhibition in the open, and I have no doubt that the assorted watchers had a more enjoyable time that morning than ever before. We were at least discreet enough not to parade ourselves in view of the cottage where most of the surveillance team were holed up, but took our problems down to the dunes.

Nathan did not have a good time. He found the weapon rather heavier than any stage sword he had ever handled, and complained about its design. It was also rather blunt and had more than a little rust near the hilt. I pointed out to him that it was probably a working weapon of purely functional aspect, and that the ones used in the duel would, in all likelihood, be clean and sharp with ornamental fingerguards. This didn't seem to soothe him much, and I could see why. Whatever else it might be, the sword was serviceable. A man who received a solid clout from it would not be getting up to look for more. It had an approximate point but it was really built for slashing—not the kind of thing you'd use for a little fancy dancing and a token prick on the arm. Even if neither of the duellists wanted to hurt the other badly an accident could very easily happen. And if one or the other lost his temper . . .

"It's all to your advantage," I told him. "The heavier the sword the slower the contest. The slower the contest the bigger the margin between his drug-induced torpor and your drug-induced vitality. He's no bigger than you are, he's no stronger than you are, he's no fitter than you are."

"But he knows how to use a sword," Nathan pointed out.

"How does he know?" I replied, with a liberal helping of scorn. "He was taught to fence, maybe. He's been in duels before. But has he ever learned to use the thing *properly*? He's been taught an elaborate ritual—move and countermove—whose purpose is to make a point, draw blood with a touch. It's almost as phoney as the way you were taught. Probably very much the same. There's nothing to worry about. Even if you did lose you'd only spill a little blood. And if I can get even money I'll put my last two years back pay down."

Needless to say, I wasn't wholly sincere in all of this, but it's the plain duty of a gentleman's second to keep up his morale with a little judicious exaggeration.

"You'll be pretty sick anyway," I continued, "when the stimulant wears off. I'm not going to stint you on it. For a couple of hours it will turn you into greased lightning, then you'll collapse and feel as sick as a parrot for a further couple of hours. You won't notice a little scratch. And if you *do* insist on getting hit, try to intercept his blade with your head. You've got a skull like an armor-plated apple and duelling scars are *so* attractive. It will do wonders for your image back on Earth."

"Not," he said, "in the circles I move in. I'd be a joke. The diplomat who couldn't talk himself out of a swordfight."

"So okay," I said, reasonably. "You'd better win, hadn't you? It's easy. You have about twenty percent on him as regards speed, maybe more. And he thinks he's a racing certainty. He'll be as cocky as hell. . . . taking it easy. You can probably get in for a quick dab and out again while he's still congratulating hmself on how good he's going to be."

"He'll get one hell of a shock if he loses," mused Nathan. "And he's an important man. Not the kind of man to make into an enemy if you can help it."

"He already is," I said, flatly. "There's no point in going into this thing still wondering whether or not to chuck it. If you want to throw the fight, decide now. Otherwise, you'll go in there in a hell of a tangle and you'll lose anyway, probably while you're deciding that it would be a good idea to win. Zarnecki is a self-appointed enemy and he won't be any more generously disposed to you if you let him cut you. Whereas if you win . . ."

"Sure," he replied. "I saw all those old movies too. Where the hero fights the leader of the savages hand-to-hand, beats him, and wins his respect and undying friendship. It doesn't work that way in real life, Alex."

"No," I said, improvising, "Zarnecki is Philip's number one boy. But he isn't a son or a brother. There are half a dozen others who'd like his spot. You make a monkey out of Zarnecki and someone else gets the plum. Someone who could hardly be anything but better disposed towards us. And, since their methods of leaning on us will then have failed, maybe they'll try a gentler tack next time.

Philip, remember, is still uninvolved so far as appearances go. He can change horses in midstream without batting a regal eyelid. If you win, you could win co-operation and you'll certainly win respect. Maybe not from Zarnecki, if he gets bitter about it, but from Philip and from some of the others."

He nodded slowly, still giving the impression of someone enmeshed by tortuous doubts. Maybe the memories of acting school had brought out a latent longing to play Hamlet.

"Look," I said, getting a little tired. "Speak now or forever hold thy goddam trap shut. We have to go back to the ship so I can fill you full of firewater. If you want to jack it in say so now, because I tell you straight that once I've shot the elixir into your veins you'll feel like going out to lick the entire world with one hand tied."

"For a peaceful man, Alex," he said, "you're taking an extremely aggressive line. What happened to your neo-Christian sympathies: avoid violence at all costs, always submit."

"I'm adaptable," I told him. "I never was a devout neo-Christian. What they say makes a little sense . . . sometimes. But I haven't forgotten that when I stood there and invited Arne Jason to blow my head off he bloody tried. I figure that if providence saves you once it isn't just so's you can make the same mistake a second time. I don't like violence and I don't like ritual violence even more. But I want you to beat Zarnecki because it's the only answer the circumstances permit. Maybe the last couple of years have allowed you to pollute my soul. I'm not as scornful of expediency as I once was."

"I suppose I really have to win," he said. "Otherwise you might find your newly lost faith in the value of rigid morality. Come on, let's go."

And with that, we went.

I gave him the shot while we still had half an hour in hand. That meant that he would be just a little over the top when the fight started, which was all to the good. I wanted to let him get used to his hyped-up condition and to lose just a little of the godlike arrogance that was likely to coincide with the first burst of superpower. I figured that Zarnecki would bring to the fight enough arrogance for two men.

By noon, when we made our way to the *rendezvous*, Nathan had already been on top of the world and was looking round for something else to engage his appetite for doing great things.

He did a lot of smiling.

Zarnecki, accompanied by Cade and another man, whose name I didn't know, met us at the appointed place—again, in the dunes, but in a kind of hollow bowl between drifts, where there was space. I didn't like the look of the soft sandy soil, but only the top had dried out following the previous night's rain and it would be firm enough.

The duelling sword *was* clean and polished, equipped with a much finer point. It even had the ornamental grip I'd predicted. Nathan made a few experimental passes while I exchanged a couple of pleasantries with Cade. He made sure that I knew the rules. There weren't very many—the most important one being the bit about stopping when blood was drawn. Zarnecki, meanwhile, stood perfectly stiff, and kept his face stern and solemn right up to the off.

As soon as the off *was* called, however, Zarnecki did allow an expression to seep into his features—a cruel and cheerful expression which might have made strong men quiver in its time. It didn't do anything to Nathan, though. He was still smiling.

I know nothing about the supposed art of sword-play, and find myself unable to give a technical and exact description of the performance. I suspect that by technical standards it was a bit of a farce and would have had Cyrano de Bergerac rolling in the aisles, but I wouldn't know the difference.

Zarnecki came forward like a dancer, on his toes, with the point of his blade making little spirals in the air as his arm moved and his wrist twisted. Nathan may have been the one with acting experience but it was Zarnecki who looked like a ham.

Zarnecki opened his attack with a forward thrust anyone could have dodged. It was purely for show. Nathan moved round it and made a quick movement of his blade that looked more like a tennis shot than an attempt at murder. Zarnecki blocked it, and went back a pace, letting Nathan follow it up. Nathan did, pivoting on his front foot and wheeling the blade round to slash from the other direction. It looked like a comic move, but I saw the shadow of surprise cross Zarnecki's face as he realized how fast Nathan had reacted. But Zarnecki blocked with ease, the blades clinking dully.

Nathan came forward, looking a little like an over-anxious lion tamer. But there was real meaning in the prods he directed at his opponent. Zarnecki had to parry and retreat, and the expression on his face was now genuine uncertainty.

I don't think that Zarnecki had intended it to be a short fight. I think he had been prepared to indulge in a little bear-baiting, trying to get Nathan into something of a temper, frustrated and furious. But he was changing his mind now about the management of the scenario.

The crowd, of course, stood silent, with all due dignity. I couldn't quite bring myself to ruin the atmosphere by cheering, but I allowed myself a grin, which I showed off to Cade and his companion by half-turning and taking my eye off the combatants for an instant.

Naturally, I missed the important play. When I looked back Zarnecki was coming forward, thrusting as though he meant it. He was putting Nathan's unexpected ability to the test now, and I saw him talk himself back into confidence as Nathan's parries were clumsy. I wanted to shout to Nathan to use his feet more and his fancy acting less, but I felt sure that he'd realize himself the way it had to be played.

The blades stopped clinking as Zarnecki ceased his attack and rocked back on his heels, giving himself a moment's rest. Nathan didn't want that, and immediately dived in—somewhat recklessly, I thought. So did Zarnecki, for he reacted swiftly, turning Nathan's blade and aiming to slip right through to strike his chest. Nathan twisted, and the point went whistling past. Without pause or any sign that it was unpremeditated, Nathan brought his arm round in a short, sharp arc so that his armoured fist struck Zarnecki on the forearm. Zarnecki didn't like it.

I wished, briefly, that I really had managed to put a bet on.

As they came apart again, making threatening gestures with the blades but not attempting to strike while they fought to regain balance and stance, the difference in speed looked obvious. Zarnecki looked far more as if he knew what he was doing, but compared to Nathan he was clumsy. There was no more than a taint of grace in the way Nathan plied his weapon—acting training or no—but it ended up where it needed to go each time, or drew a parry from Zarnecki.

I glanced round again. The home team weren't liking it. That made me feel even better.

Zarnecki was stiff now, and something mechanical got into his movements. He was too self-conscious, thinking hard about what he was doing. He had lost his natural flow. There was no longer any question of cat and mouse. Zarnecki went in again intending to end it as soon as was humanly possible.

But it wasn't.

Nathan had allowed the advantage of surprise to wear off, and that should have counted against him. But it didn't. Zarnecki under pressure became a different man. He was all veneer and his veneer had cracked—not because of anything real that Nàthan had achieved but simply because his own plans had gone awry.

As we'd noted, duelling *meant* something on Wildeblood. Zarnecki stood to lose ... not just the fight, but—or so it must have seemed to him—everything. He couldn't stand that thought. Losing was something alien to him, and it was a subject on which he was very brittle.

I'm sure he could have done better than he did. But there was desperation in the way he went at Nathan, and not too much style. There was a force in the cuts he directed at Nathan but no real guts. Nathan only had to catch a couple with his blade. The rest he moved away from with too much of a comfortable margin. Curiously, though—or perhaps not so curiously—Zarnecki was still aiming to draw a superficial stripe in Nathan's flesh. There was no sign of murder in the thrusts.

It was exactly the situation in which Nathan's unnatural superiority could show to good advantage, and if Nathan seemed horribly labored in capitalizing on his speed it was probably the unreasonable demands of my imagination which made him seem so. An awfully long time seemed to go by while Zarnecki forced him back and prompted him into an agitated dance.

But all of a sudden it was over. Zarnecki reached

too far, completely underestimating the distance that Nathan could cover in a couple of seconds. Left exposed while he groped, he could only try to bring up his left arm when Nathan moved round and in. The hand wasn't enough. Nathan's point slipped under it and whipped across. The strike was lower than Nathan had intended—beneath the lower rib—but he had judged the range of the slash accurately. There appeared a fifteen inch gash in Zarnecki's shirt, and blood spilled from the cut. The abdominal wall was hardly pricked and there was no damage to the intestine. But it must have hurt like hell.

For just an instant I thought that Zarnecki was so far gone in anger and anguish that he wouldn't leave it. But conditioned response triumphed and his sword sagged. He didn't cry out, but when Nathan stepped back Zarnecki reeled. He jabbed the sword point into the sand, but couldn't or wouldn't support himself as if it were a stick. He sank instead to one knee.

I found, slightly to my surprise, that the fear which had suddenly arisen and was now draining away was the fear that Nathan might have had to kill him.

There was a look on the defeated man's face that can only be described as horror. He got up again from his half-kneeling position but sat down. He laid the sword at his side and tried to pull the cut edges of his shirt apart to inspect the damage. Cade and the other man went to help him. I went too, but when I bent down, reaching out to the wound, they all turned on me. I could almost feel the shame and disgust that were welling up in Zarnecki despite his attempts to keep them down.

I could tell that he wasn't in the market for immediate treatment. I could also tell that there was no emergency. I left it, stepping back. Zarnecki's

eyes followed me. He was staring at me, and I realized that the venom in his stare was all for me. He
needed someone to hate, just then . . . someone to
blame. He couldn't turn his bitterness on Nathan,
because that was forbidden in his way of thinking.
But I was a candidate. Hadn't I already exposed
myself as less than a gentleman? He didn't know
that it was me that had given Nathan the ability to
win the fight, and so he didn't know that I was, in
a way, to blame for his defeat. But that made no
difference. I was there. I was available.

In a way, it was almost justice, of a kind.

It was Cade who found something to say.

"It is settled," he pronounced, ritually.

I nodded, quelling a temptation to agree in less
than formal fashion.

"It will not be recalled and never spoken," he
added.

"Naturally," I said. I tried not to sound sarcastic.

We packed up and parted. They'd brought both
swords but they didn't bother to pick up either.
Nathan's was tainted and the other was a loser. Apparently, they were what passed for the spoils. I
collected them, and offered them to Nathan hilt
first.

"Take your pick," I said. "Souvenir. You could
hang it on your cabin wall. Or maybe wear it."

He took one, and broke the blade across his
knee. It was the one with blood on it—just the
merest trace, at the point.

I looked surprised.

"We've done no good here," he said. "There was
no good to be done. It's over now, let's all try to
forget it."

He seemed to be coming down faster than I'd
anticipated. He wasn't supposed to come over
queer for another hour yet. But circumstances can
alter cases.

"It was me who got the basilisk stare," I said. "I don't much mind being *persona non grata*. You can still do your job, I can still do mine."

"It's not your fault," he agreed. "We both did what we could. But we have an enemy there, and if his position is put in jeopardy by his failure he could be dangerous. No one gives up the kind of power he has gracefully, aristocratic upbringing or no."

We walked back to the ship, not too rapidly. I caught sight of one of our shadows dutifully tailing along.

"I have to win Philip over," he said. "No one else ... though a friend at court might help. I have to show him that we aren't a threat. *Show* him ... instead of just telling him."

"Invite him to the *Daedalus*," I suggested, wanly. "We'll throw a party and get him maudlin drunk."

"I think we need the key to that code," he said.

"We've known that for days," I pointed out. "*Everybody* needs the key to the code. But once we've cracked it we might not be *able* to give it to Philip as a token of our hypocritical esteem. It might be dynamite. Messages are put into code to stop people from finding out what's in them, and there's usually a reason. Of all the people we know, Philip's the one who's most likely not to like what's in the message—because he's the one who'd certainly know the answer if he was meant to be able to read it."

"Maybe he already knows it," said Nathan. "Maybe he's supposed to know it but doesn't because of some historical accident."

"One of the great granddaddies was meant to pass it on, no doubt," I commented, "and he didn't quite have time for his famous last words. Said: 'The secret is ...' and clapped out. Hardly. As a theory, that's bullshit."

"So are all the other theories I can think of," he said. "When you have eliminated the bullshit, and nothing remains . . ."

"Then you're in a pretty shitty situation," I answered for him.

Silence fell, for a little while. We reached the ship and I took Nathan straight to the lab for a shot to counteract the one he'd already had.

"It won't subvert the reaction entirely," I warned him, "but it'll help."

I escorted him back to his cabin, and sat down on the bed to keep him company while he began to feel sick. I wanted to make sure there wouldn't be any complications from the speed-up stuff, and to reassure him that there weren't even if there were.

"You don't like the setup here, do you?" he asked.

I shook my head.

"It's a successful colony," he said. "Established, expanding, developing. This feudal setup is just a phase, and in any case it's half-hearted tyranny at worst. Economic development will destroy the Wildeblood dynasty—or force it to adapt. The drug doesn't really figure as a secure power base in the long run."

I shrugged. "Am I making waves?" I asked. "I'll sit tight while you nurse Philip's anxieties. I don't mind our being friends. I guess I'd rather things were this way than find another Dendra. But don't ask me to like it. That's too much."

"Deep down," he said, "you'd really like to give your melodramatic friend the answers he wants, wouldn't you?"

"I don't want to start a war."

"But you do want to kick the brick out from under Philip?"

"I can't have it both ways, can I?" I asked him, still speaking levelly. "I never can. That's the way it goes. We all have to compromise. But the setup here worries me. And you worry me, because I think that deep down—maybe as deep as my feelings—you like this place. You like the way Wildeblood set it up. It appeals to you. Not in the sense that you'd like to stay here as the power behind the throne, or that you might like to set yourself up with one just like it . . . it's something more subtle than that. The idea of manipulating people appeals to you. You admire Wildeblood, just as you admired the Planners on Floria and the UN back home. Basically, you don't have any belief in what we're out here trying to do. You're just a professional, you say, doing your job. I worry about that professionalism, because I worry about what kind of job you think you're doing and how you intend to work it. I believe, now, that you will work it, in the long run . . . but for the right reasons. For personal satisfaction and reputation—maybe even a kind of glory. I don't trust you, Nathan, any more than I could trust Philip or Zarnecki. I can't."

"That's straight talking," he said. "Anyone would think you'd just been watching a sword-fight. Is that what let it all out?"

"Maybe," I conceded.

"Shall I tell you what you're really afraid of?" he asked, suavely. Then, without waiting for an answer, he went on: "What you're really afraid of isn't the conclusion I might reach as a result of studying this colony and the others we've visited—it's the fact that *you* might be driven to a similar conclusion. You're scared that your experiences out here might point your deadly analytical mind to a series of answers that conflict with your precious and deep-seated beliefs. You're beginning to bury those beliefs and the holier-than-thou attitude you once had with them, but you're nowhere near relinquishing them. You're still a neo-Christian in your gut no matter how far your head guides your actions away from it. What frightens you . . . deep down . . . is the possibility that you might not find any excuse to disagree with me in regard to the report I make to Pietrasante. Right?"

"I suppose," I commented. "That you expect me to say: 'touché'."

"Not really," he replied. "But think about it."

He was beginning to look a little grey about the face, and his voice sounded tired.

I couldn't help feeling that it served him right.

12

Ⅎ

While Nathan was recovering, I called Conrad. I told him the result of the fight, and brought him up to date on the situation in general. He was suitably unimpressed.

"We're still on schedule," he reported. "They're used to our being around now, and showing signs of curiosity. We've got some good film of one or two sign conversations—which is difficult, because it means getting cameras lined up two different ways and then reintegrating the film to catch both sides. One big advantage of talking is that you don't have to keep your eyes on the other guy's fingers . . . makes the whole business of communication less absorbing and less distracting. Mariel still says she's making progress, although she's not specific about what and how. I think she just *feels* that she's in with a chance. I'll back her."

"I hate to say this," I told him, "but there's a possibility we'll have to move out. The atmosphere is tense. I'm certain Zarnecki wants to be rid of us, one way or another. If he can persuade Philip, and he's a good deal closer to Philip's ear than we are . . ."

"If we have to pull out, Alex," he said, soberly, "it will be a catastrophe."

"I know that," I told him.

"It's been well over a hundred years," he said. "Of all the intelligent alien races we've contacted, this is the first we've ever had a real chance to get to know. This is *important*, Alex—incomparably more important than colony politics or Earth politics or what the hell."

"I *know*," I repeated. "But these are the circumstances under which we live. The UN didn't vote funds for chatting to alien primitives about their philosophies of life. They voted funds for very ordinary, very mundane concerns like investigating colonies to see whether it might be worth trying to reinstitute a space program. Without that space program, it's dubious that we'll *ever* get a chance to chat with aliens again. The mission comes first."

"Couldn't you just leave the island? If you and Nathan were to come here too. . . ."

"We couldn't bring the ship. That would be wasting resources. And in any case, it won't work. We need the good will of the colony to keep working here. They're suspicious now—how would they be if we all retired to some desolate spot to start trying to communicate with the indigenes? They wouldn't understand that—they probably wouldn't even believe it. They don't have anything to do with the aliens—it's strictly live and let live. They can't understand our interest in them—they don't have your priorities."

"Why not?" Conrad returned.

It wasn't an answer I'd expected. It wasn't something I'd thought about. What he meant was: *why* didn't the colony have his priorities. It was something I'd just taken for granted before, as something which simply *was*. But why? All of a sudden, it did seem odd.

"James Wildeblood was a biologist," said Conrad. "He must have been personally interested in contact with the aliens. He must have been aware of the significance of contact."

"And yet," I said, "he had it built into the law that there should be no interference ... Alice told me that the other night. Perhaps he was trying to protect the salamen from his descendants."

"He doesn't seem to have been concerned with protecting anything else from his descendants," Conrad pointed out.

"Perhaps it's precisely because he was a biologist that he made this particular exception," I suggested.

Once again we were back to the question: What kind of a man was Wildeblood?

It wasn't difficult to understand why he'd never made any attempt personally to open communications with the salamen. He'd had plenty to occupy his time without that. The same went for the whole colony, they had a world to build. But now, with a small but apparently not overworked aristocracy running a colony that was more than sustaining itself . . . why not? Simply because their thoughts hadn't turned that way, it seemed. And why not? Because James Wildeblood had put nothing in his scheme that would encourage thoughts to turn that way. In all likelihood ninety-nine people out of a hundred didn't even know that the salamen existed, or care.

Eventually, I said: "It doesn't mean anything. It's just something that was left aside."

"It would be a terrible tragedy," said Conrad, "if we were expelled from this world now. Quite apart from the fact that we'll have missed an opportunity . . . have you thought about what might happen when the colonists *do* rediscover the salamen? Especially if the Wildeblood oligarchy is still in power. They could be ripe for exploitation—colonialism in the ancient sense."

"It had occurred to me," I admitted. And maybe, my thought ran on, that's why James Wildeblood didn't draw attention to the existence of intelligent natives here, but allowed—or encouraged—the fact to be forgotten. Maybe he *did* know a very great

119

deal about the significance of human contact with aliens . . . in the wrong circumstances. I didn't find it hard to believe that James Wildeblood might have had far more conscience when it came to dealing with aliens than he had when it was a matter of dealing with fellow humans.

"You have to fight," said Conrad. "You and Nathan. It's up to you to keep us here. You must."

"We're doing our best," I said. "We can't do more. As soon as Nathan wakes up it's once more into the breach, and only time will tell whether or not we've blown the whole thing."

I signed off.

I went back to find out whether Nathan had overcome the reaction against the stimulant I'd given him earlier. He hadn't, quite. He was awake, but he was still lying flat out on his bunk. I made as if to leave again, but he stopped me before I could open the door.

"About what I said earlier, Alex," he said. "I'm sorry. I ran away with myself. It was the after-effects coming on. Not just the drug . . . the fight. I was pretty tight about it, you know."

"It's okay," I said.

"I didn't mean it," he said, making sure. I didn't know quite how to take it. Looked at uncharitably, the more in control of himself he was, the more likely he was to be lying. He'd meant what he said . . . then. But now he was taking time out to apologize, which was fair.

"Did you ever hear the old saw about the mechanic and the dent?" I asked.

"Probably," he said. "But go ahead."

"Guy with a new car bumps it while he's parking. The wing's fancy aluminium, no tensile strength to speak of . . . it isn't much of a bump but it leaves a big dent . . . very unsightly. So he takes it to the mechanic, who looks at the dent for a couple of minutes, sizing it up from six different angles. Then he bends down and thumps the wing further along with the heel of his hand. The dent springs back out, leaving the wing good as new. The mechanic says: 'That's ten dollars,' and the owner says: 'How the hell do you figure that? All you did was hit the damn thing with your hand.' So the mechanic makes out an itemized account. It says: *One tap with hand, two cents; knowing where to tap, nine dollars ninety-eight.* See?"

It was an old story. It had probably been around in the days of the model T.

Nathan didn't take long to catch on.

"What you're saying," he said. "is that this colony has succeeded not because Wildeblood was a dictator but because he was an ecologist. It wasn't the way he went about it that mattered, just the fact that he knew what needed to be done."

"It's worth considering," I said.

"So every colony should have an ecologist in charge?"

"An ecologist of Wildeblood's calibre."

"Do you believe that? Is that the reason this colony came off, in your mind?"

"What has belief got to do with it?" I asked, with heavy irony. "What matters is the story we give to the UN. That could be mine. I might stick to it. How about you?"

He grinned. "I'll think it over," he promised. "I think I feel better now. Does our carriage await?"

"There's one at the cottage," I said. "I'll signal them."

I went out to do just that.

The carriage provided for our use this time was a rather different affair from the one that had been ambushed the night before. It had four wheels, two horses and seated six. Sitting beside the driver, on the elevated section at the front, was a man with a rifle. Neither Elkanah nor Miranda was on duty—both for fairly obvious reasons. Neither the servant that was driving nor the guard had much in the line of conversation, and so the drive passed without much to enliven the time.

Supper at the house' was a less than merry meal. There were, if I counted right, thirteen at table, but I don't think that had a lot to do with it. Zarnecki was there, at Philip's right hand, looking very much in control of himself and the situation. I was seated between an old lady and Cade, as I had been for most meals. We'd discovered weeks ago that we didn't have anything in common. There was nothing in the air to mark the supper apart from others we'd enjoyed (if that's the right word) at the same table. The daggers might be drawn but they were kept very much out of sight. Under the tablecloth, I supposed.

All through the evening, in fact, the facade was maintained, although it took effort on my part and, in all probability, even more effort on the part of Zarnecki. Only Nathan had the equipment ready on hand to oil his way through the maze of potential thorns. He was charming to Alice and respectful to Philip, and it seemed to me that he was a prime candidate for another seduction charge.

I was glad enough to get up to my room and lie down for a while preparatory to my scheduled dead-of-night adventure. It was getting to be a habit.

I followed exactly the same procedure as I had on the earlier occasion, waiting until I was reasonably sure that the household was as still as it was going to be, and then tiptoeing through the corridors to the back stairs. I made for the same door, and everything went perfectly . . . until I reached it.

It was locked. And someone had taken care to remove the key. Extra security precautions seemed to be in force—or perhaps I had just been lucky the first time.

I cursed silently, and made my way back to the main part of the house. But there I found the hall still lighted, and I already knew that the heavy bolts on the front door would take some drawing. Opening the massive thing without undue noise would be one hell of a trick.

After a couple of minutes' thought I decided that my best bet lay not in the main section at all, but out in the desolate quiet of the west wing. There might not be any unlocked doors there—none that I could locate, anyhow—but I was pretty sure I could find the museum gallery even in the dark. And it wouldn't matter if I fumbled a bit, because no one was likely to see or hear. There were plenty of windows in that gallery.

And so I proceeded to feel my way through the darkened corridors, taking my time, and feeling quite relaxed. I located the door of the hall where James Wildeblood had established his collection, and opened it carefully. The noise it made seemed loud and penetrating to me, but I slipped inside and stood perfectly still, ears straining to catch the faintest sound that might signal pursuit. There was nothing.

I worked my way along the wall, testing the windows as I came to them. Alternate ones were built to open, but the first two I tried were firmly stuck. The third one, however, gave as I tugged, and slid up with no more than the merest groan. I swung myself over the sill, and began to let the window down behind me. Then, as an afterthought, I picked up a pebble and used it to wedge the window, preventing it from closing fully. The crack that remained was not obvious but I could get my fingers into it. I would have no trouble getting back in again.

I moved along the inner wall of the west wing, toward the open edge of the courtyard. When I reached the end of the building I crouched down and breathed deeply for a few minutes while I measured the open expanse of lawn that separated me from the railing. It was a starry night and my eyes were well used to the dark by now. I wouldn't need a flashlight—which was perhaps as well, in view of the fact that the man I was going to meet had mine already in his possession.

I decided that I didn't like the look of the open space. Everything seemed quiet, but if there was a guard anywhere he would likely be at the gate, and while I crossed the lawn I would be visible.

Instead, I worked my way around to the other side—the outer wall—of the wing, intending to use the cover of the gardens and outhouses at the back. All went well until I cut away from the shadow of the house and sprinted for the nearest of the outbuildings. Somewhere ahead of me a dog began to bark.

I turned, instantly, and began to run away from the sound. I had covered twenty yards or so when I heard a voice, and a light showed as a door was opened somewhere in the cluster of huts and barns. I threw myself flat. There was hardly any cover—I was in grass that was none-too-long, some distance from the nearest tree. But they were coming out of a lighted room . . . they wouldn't pick me out if I didn't move.

But that wasn't the danger.

The barking started up again—and this time it was coming closer. They had released the dog.

I got up and sprinted for the nearest section of iron rail. But I hadn't a chance. I had well over a hundred yards to cover and I had barely a couple of seconds start on the dog. It caught up with me in the open and dived for my heels. I spun and stumbled, and then could do nothing except protect my face from the dog. It darted in and out, snarling and yapping, but it didn't try to tear me to bits. It had done its job. It didn't have to bite and hadn't been trained to.

A couple of minutes passed while they caught up. It seemed like a long time. I was grateful when it ended and the handler silenced the dog with a couple of blows with the end of its leash. Then there was another pause while someone brought up a light. I didn't try anything. There were three of them and they still had the dog. I just came slowly to my feet, moving very carefully.

By the time the lantern came I had decided that my only way out was a strong piece of bluff.

"What the hell is going on?" I demanded. "Philip will have your hides for this! Setting the dogs on his guests, by God...!"

It didn't sound convincing, even to me. And when the light arrived and I saw who was coming after it my heart sank. The lantern was being carried by the blond servant who'd followed me a couple of days back, and with him was Zarnecki—fully dressed and obviously not recently risen from his bed.

"Out walking, Mr. Alexander?" he asked.

"Of course I was," I replied, trying to make it sound like a perfectly natural thing to be doing. "I couldn't sleep."

"You know better than to wander about after dark," he said. "There are thieves about, remember?"

"I wasn't going outside the grounds," I lied, valiantly. "I thought I'd be safe here. I didn't realize that you had dog patrols and machine-gun emplacements."

The scorn and sarcasm bounced off.

"Had you told us that you wanted to take a

stroll," he murmured, with mock courtesy, "we would have made arrangements. As it was, you see, the very precautions undertaken for your protection . . ."

He left the sentence hanging.

"I notice you haven't been sleeping yourself," I countered. "Maybe it's the change in the weather?"

"Perhaps it is," he said. "But I wasn't intending to sleep tonight. I thought that if the occasion arose I might like to do a little hunting."

"And has it?" I asked.

"I think so," he said. Then, to one of the servants who had come out after the dog, he said: "Rouse the rest of the men. Get the dogs out. Shielded lanterns. Send a runner to the *gendarmerie* and tell Beloff to get his men in position. You cover the dunes. Cade and the farmers' men will look after the fields to the east and north. I'll take the cemetery and the woods with the larger pack of dogs."

He turned back to me then.

"I think we may catch our thieves," he said.

"I hope you're not going to this trouble on my account," I said.

The dog was being led away now, and the servants were retiring with it at the double. Only Zarnecki and the blond man remained. I knew I could outrun Zarnecki, but there seemed to be no point now. I couldn't get to the cemetery in time to warn the man with the big nose, and there was still a chance I could brazen it out with Zarnecki.

But Zarnecki took the lantern then.

"Search him," he said, briefly.

The blond youth made a move toward my pockets. I dropped my hands and backed away slightly.

"What the hell do you think you're playing at?" I demanded.

"I want to see what you have in your pockets," Zarnecki replied, calmly.

126

In all probability, he didn't know what he was looking for. But I had only one thing in my pockets, and that was one thing I didn't want him to find.

"You can't do this," I said, feeling the absurd falseness of the line so bitterly that I left the last two words out.

He shrugged. "Let's go back to the house, then," he said. "And we'll find out then what we can do and what we can't."

I knew I was on to a loser. In circumstances such as these, no appeal to Philip could possibly succeed, even if Zarnecki *was* on the brink of falling out of favour. I reached into my pocket and produced the folded piece of paper.

"All I have is this," I said, calmly.

He fumbled it open with one hand, holding the lantern aloft with the other.

"Where did you get this?" he demanded, when he had looked at it. His voice was firm and confident.

"It's a copy of the one Miranda gave to Nathan," I said. "I think you know that very well."

It didn't come off.

"This is paper from our factory, Mr. Alexander," he said. "Isn't it strange that you should make your copies on our paper."

"Hardly," I said. "We don't carry vast stocks aboard the *Daedalus*. Every gram counts. Naturally we took steps to procure some of your paper."

He didn't bother to ask who had given it to us. He had already decided not to believe me. He hadn't the time to waste in proving that I wasn't innocent.

"Go back to your room, Mr. Alexander," he said. "I have work to do. But stay there. We'll be wanting you again. There's nowhere you can run to."

I shrugged. "If that's what you want," I said. "But you're making a mountain out of a molehill."

Stick with it to the bitter end, I thought.

Unfortunately, I had a feeling that the bitter end was only just around the corner.

It's up to you, Cyrano, I muttered under my breath. Somehow, you have to get away.

13

But he didn't get away.

I knew he hadn't when they came back to my room, half an hour or so after dawn.

I'd watched the dawn from the windows of my room. I hadn't been able to sleep. I'd seen the dregs of the search parties begin to trickle in after their hard night's work: Men, dogs, horses, all looking tired. There were a lot of them. I hadn't realized what kind of an operation Zarnecki had planned. It occurred to me that he'd have looked a bit of a fool if nothing had happened. Maybe this was his way of redeeming himself for the duelling fiasco. Maybe it had been something of a desperate play on his behalf.

I hated myself for having helped him bring it off.

He came into my room with Cade and Elkanah. The blond youth, who had been sitting outside the door all night, hovered in the background.

He looked me over. I was still dressed. I guess I looked a little rumpled after my little short-circuited adventure. He still looked very composed, and quite neat. A night's arduous hunting seemed to have made little or no impression on him. But he was wearing an attitude of triumph that gave him a lot of help.

"You're under arrest, Mr. Alexander," he said.

"Where's Philip?" I demanded.

"Philip's asleep," replied Zarnecki. "There really is no point in waking him."

"In that case," I said, "I want to see Nathan."

"He can visit you in jail," Zarnecki promised.

His tone was aggressive, even insulting. He thought he had me exactly where he wanted me. I was afraid that he might be right.

"What's the charge?" I asked, harshly. "And where's your evidence?"

He was ready for those questions all right.

"Treasonous conspiracy," he said. "And as for evidence, we have a copy of a coded message with the first few numbers missing . . . the numbers which were written on the piece of paper *you* had, apparently in the same handwriting. And we have a torch and a wristwatch. All these things were found in the possession of a man we caught on the hill on the far side of the cemetery. He had, it seems, been waiting for someone to meet him. And you, Mr. Alexander, appeared to be going somewhere tonight when we interrupted you."

Put like that, it looked like two and two adding to four. It had its weak points. The stolen flashlight and the watch didn't mean a thing. And no one could prove that either of us was heading for a midnight tryst. But the two parts of the coded message . . .

Zarnecki, at any rate, thought I was a dead duck. He wasn't even bothering to wake Philip. Come morning, the whole thing would be *fait accompli*. And Nathan was really going to have to put in some work to try and get me off.

If the duel had been one up to us, the score was level now, and no mistake.

"Come on," said Cade.

I went.

"What's the penalty?" I asked, as we went down the staircase.

"We'll settle for exile, I think," said Zarnecki.

I wasn't surprised. I also wasn't confident that he wouldn't get away with it. In all probability, Nathan and Pete Rolving would figure that retirement from the scene was the only way out. The situation on the mainland—Conrad's priorities—wouldn't count for much now.

They took me to jail in a closed carriage. I didn't enjoy the ride. The sun was getting up and the sky was cloudless. It looked like another fine day. I didn't suppose I'd get much joy out of it where I was going.

The jailhouse was a squat, square stone building that seemed a little lonely, set somewhere out to the west of the town, hidden from the road by an embankment. There wasn't much inside except half a dozen cells with dirty walls and iron bars set in the heavy doors and the windows.

I judged that the local crime rate wasn't a severe problem. Only one of the cells was occupied, and that was by a tall man with an outsize pointed nose.

They put us in together.

I wasn't quite sure how to play it. Should I admit that the game was up and acknowledge him, or keep my cards closed despite the fact that they knew what kind of hand I held? He didn't give me any lead, and I could feel his eyes watching me from behind even after the bolts slid home.

In the end, I decided to stick it out.

"Hi," I said. "Are you the guy they caught with my watch and torch or are you the local horse-thief?"

He gave me a dirty look and didn't answer.

I couldn't figure out whether he was acting or whether that was his authentic reaction. Probably both.

The room had three bunks—two doubled up and one set at right-angles under the window. He was lying on the odd one. I sat down on the bottom one of the pair, testing it for comfort. It was hard—the mattress was filled with straw—and didn't

seem the ideal spot for catching up on a bad night.
I stayed sitting.

The faces beyond the iron panel disappeared, and
I heard the footsteps marching all the way along
the stone corridor to the door. Unless they'd left an
eavesdropping dwarf outside we were alone.

The wandering minstrel apparently figured we
could talk safely now.

"They came with a pack of dogs," he said. "I
couldn't get to the town or the big wood. Did they
know where I was?"

"I don't think so," I told him. "They intercepted
me before I got out of the grounds. They mounted
a big operation—they had the countryside covered
for miles around. I guess they knew anyone I was
going to meet couldn't be too far away. I didn't tell
them anything, but Zarnecki was already suspicious.
Maybe he spotted the robbery was a phoney."

"It was too soon," said the big man.

I agreed with him. His voice wasn't accusatory,
but I knew it was my fault. I'd hustled for the rest
of the code. If only we'd had time in hand . . .

"What happens now?" I asked.

"They'll send me to a coal mine somewhere," he
said. "I'll get away. Then I'll carry on. I can get
help. People will hide me, feed me, supply me."

He didn't mention me. I don't think he cared.
He'd already accepted that he'd lost this round, and
that the next would have to take place on the same
old ground. He'd written off this particular ploy to
experience.

I was grateful that at least he wasn't angry.

"Ah well," I said. "Time on my hands at last. If I
still had the code I could have another go at crack-
ing it. But Zarnecki took it all. I take it your people
have another copy?"

"We can get one," he said.

"Zarnecki wanted us to bust the code for him,

too," I remarked, conversationally. "He gave Nathan the first few numbers . . . just about as much as you gave me."

He didn't seem surprised. "Why didn't you ask *him* for the rest?" he asked, a little sourly.

"He didn't give the impression of wanting the answer that badly," I replied. I was thinking, meanwhile, that Nathan might well ask to see the rest. And if he *could* decipher it then maybe we still had something left to bargain with.

"I still don't understand this business about the code," I said, after a pause. "It seems such a crude and stupid thing for a man like Wildeblood to have done. How did he ever expect the eventual decoding to be done? Obviously it's immune to trial and error or someone would have got it years ago. There's obviously a trick to it. But what's the point of using a trick unless you're pretty confident that whoever it's intended for will be able to spot the trick? None of it makes sense."

I was just talking for the sake of talking, filling in time while I reflected on what a sad and sorry business it was all round. It *didn't* make any sense.

Then a thought struck me.

It was a silly thought, but it suddenly seemed a little less than silly. Because, in a way, it *did* make a strange kind of sense.

Suppose that the message was intended for *me*.

Not me personally, of course . . . but someone like me. Someone from Earth. Someone come to check up on the colony, see how it was getting along. Someone with the same kind of background and knowledge as James Wildeblood.

After all, he had made his message secret. It was secret even from his family. I didn't believe that crud about it being the secret of the wonder drug, deliberately half-betrayed to incorporate a modicum of built-in obsolescence to his dynasty. That

133

wasn't credible. But suppose that there was something that James Wildeblood wanted to report back to Earth. Something about the colony that the colony didn't want to know ... and that he didn't want the colony to know. It had made everybody curious, my nameless friend and Philip's crew both, but they hadn't been able to find the trick. Maybe it wasn't the kind of thing that was incorporated into their practical brand of education.

I couldn't for the life of me imagine what such a message might contain. But I *did* guess, almost immediately, the kind of code he might have used.

The only trouble was that I no longer had my copy.

"Hey," I said. "You've lived with the damn code for years. What was the first number?"

"688668," said the big man. "Why?"

I thought hard. I turned over on the bunk, and scratched the number on the dirt that was all over the wall with the end of my thumbnail.

Right, I thought. C-double-O-double-C...

But that was wrong. Silently, I tried C-R-A-C, then put in a D-Y- instead of the second C ... but still it wasn't there.

Then I tried again, and got C-O-R-N-E-R, and I knew I'd cracked it.

It was one hell of a messy code, but it worked.

"Give me the next one," I said.

"Why?" he repeated.

"Just tell me what it is."

But he sat up now. There wasn't going to be any fooling him. And it was too late to back down. "You know it," he said.

I didn't see any point in denying it. In truth, I didn't want to deny it. I wasn't feeling too fond of Zarnecki at that particular moment. Why the hell, I asked myself, should I keep secrets just to spite their opposition? And in any case, I no longer believed that the answer might be as useful to the big man as he hoped.

"All right," I said. "I'll trade you. Give me as much as you remember and I'll tell you what the words mean. The first one is 'corner'. Now what's the second number?"

"585775," he told me. He was watching me like a hawk, no longer relaxed in acceptance of the situation.

It didn't take long to figure out that that one didn't work whichever way I combined the numbers. I opened my mouth to tell him his memory was all to cock, and then I remembered the limitations of the code. Not every combination of letters could be translated. To get his message over he'd have to take some liberties with spelling.

"That's 'cellar'," I said, thinking back. "It's spelt C-E-L-A-R-E, but it's 'cellar' all right. Next."

"971875."

That one was a bastard. I finally worked it out as 'floor'. Spelt F-L-U-O-R-E. Personally I'd have put an extra 8 in to help potential decoders, but that wasn't important. I gave my progress report to the big man, and he gave me two numbers: 7 and 74. They were easy, and quite unambiguous.

"They're just letters," I told him. "N and W."

He didn't have to be a genius to figure out that N and W stood for north-west. It was coming out nicely. But then the catch came.

"I'm not going to tell you any more," he said. "Not until you tell me how you're doing it. I want the key."

It was a pretty logical move. In his place, I'd have done the same.

"Tell me the entire message," I said, "and I'll decode it all. What does it matter what the key is?"

"I want the key," he said, flatly.

"But if I give you the key," I pointed out. "You

wouldn't need to give me any more numbers. You didn't want to give me the whole code in the first place."

But now he was angry. He got off his bunk and leaned against the one above mine. He peered down at me, and his bulk seemed to fill the space that side of the bed.

"I trusted you," he said. "It's because I trusted you and because I took a risk to bring you the rest of the message that I'm here. Now *give me the key*!"

I could see his point. In fact, I sympathized.

The hell with it, I thought.

"The key," I said, "is something called the periodic table of the elements. Chemical elements have symbols that conventionally represent them—one letter or two. They also have atomic numbers varying between one and a hundred-and-thirty-odd. Wildeblood just transcribed his message into atomic numbers, buggering about with the spelling wherever he couldn't get an accurate transcription. Theoretical chemistry isn't taught in your schools—not even to the privileged. But the table is in the material that was brought from Earth ... in virtually every text on chemistry. All you have to do is find it. You won't have any trouble stealing it ... Zarnecki and company don't know what to protect ... and they can't hide or destroy it without locking away or burning a whole section of the library tapes—one of the ones that's potentially most valuable. Anyone could have cracked the code during these last hundred years and more, if only they'd known where to look, if they'd only known what sort of thing to look *for*. Now ... what's the next number?"

"I can't remember," he said.

"Come on," I said. "We're trusting one another, remember?"

136

"I don't remember," he insisted. "I just don't know. Sure, I've looked at the thing countless times. But all that sticks in my mind is the first few...."

I had to accept it. It was very probably true.

I went back over what I already had. *Corner cellar floor north-west.* It wasn't a lot. Even the punctuation could go one of three ways. But with what I already knew or suspected it had to refer to the house. A corner of a cellar floor at the north-west of the cellar complex underneath the house. It looked possible. The west wing, where nobody went....

"All right," I conceded. "Then that's it. You have your key. I hope it's useful. I really do. Have a nice revolution, when they let you out ..."

After that, there seemed to be little else left to do, for the time being. He moved back to his own bunk, and lay down. I let myself relax, wondering futilely what James Wildeblood could possibly have wanted to say—to us—or possibly to any man, local or stranger, who knew a little science....

It must have been a stupid question, because it put me to sleep.

14

I didn't sleep deeply, but remained suspended between consciousness and unconsciousness, half aware of noises outside the building and the rustling every time the big man turned over on his bunk. A long time passed, though, before I realized that he was turning over a little more often than seemed wholly reasonable. When the knowledge of his agitation did dawn on me, I lifted my head from the pallet to look at him.

He was lying on his back, with that great jutting nose pointing up into the empty air. There was a lot of sweat on his face, and his breathing was ragged. He didn't actually look tortured, but he was far from comfortable.

At first I thought he might be ill, but then I remembered the drug. He probably hadn't had his dose for some time. He was exhibiting withdrawal symptoms.

I got up and banged on the cell door. But the sound of the banging simply echoed in the corridor, drawing no sign of response. I didn't even know whether there was anyone in the building ... they seemed to take a rather casual attitude to their prisoners in these parts.

There wasn't much I could do to help him. But I didn't like to go back to sleep. I sat on the edge of the bunk and watched him. He didn't get any worse, or any better. He glanced my way a few times, but didn't say anything. I guessed that he had been through it before. He knew what was ahead of him. It occurred to me that this might well be part of the routine softening-up process. So far, they hadn't shown much interest in him ... but it seemed likely that they might start soon. When he got into a situation of some desperation, delivered there by convenient circumstance, they might easily persuade him to relinquish a little information about who he was and how far his anti-establishment activities extended.

Eventually, the long-anticipated footfalls in the outer corridor were heard. I was off the bed waiting when the door opened. Four men came in. One was Cade, and two were *gendarmes*. The fourth was Nathan.

Cade went over to the bed, looked down at the big man briefly, then signalled his two companions and went out again. I moved to protest, but I was looking at Nathan and he signalled to me to be quiet. I didn't want to, but I did as I was told. I didn't want to jeopardize my own chances of getting out by making a fruitless demonstration.

They closed the door behind them, but didn't bolt it.

"Well?" I said, to Nathan.

He didn't waste time with recriminations. He knew what I'd been doing and he knew that my getting caught was just a bad break.

"I think I can get you out," he said. "Philip's a reasonable man, and so's Zarnecki now that he thinks he has command over the situation. All that they're demanding is that we go—as soon as humanly possible—plus a few assurances that they and I both know to be fairly meaningless. They're satisfied that we've done enough here to be able to take a fairly full report back to Earth—a report which will show this colony in a favorable light. They're satisfied that they haven't clamped down on us so hard as to make it clear that there's something here they're very keen on keeping a secret. They know we have nothing but a bagful of suspicions."

I wanted to tell him that maybe we had more than that now, but I didn't dare. Cade was just outside the door, eavesdropping dutifully. I daren't broadcast to the world that we had the key to the code. Nathan might be able to use the information later, after I'd been released. There was no hurry.

Or so I thought.

"How long is it going to take?" I asked.

"Not long," he assured me. "They aren't interested in keeping you here just for the fun of it. But they want me to recall Conrad's party now, and they don't want any stalling. I think they'll hang on to you until everything else is set and we're ready to depart."

It wasn't very welcome news. The cell wasn't the place I'd have selected to stay for my last few days on Poseidon. And with all due respect to my nameless acquaintance the company wasn't up to much either.

"I suppose I do get fed?" I said.

"You'll be okay," he assured me, serenely. "I'm sorry about the way it's turning out, but there don't seem to be many options open. They'd have found an excuse ... one way or another."

"Could you possibly negotiate for my removal to slightly less unpleasant surroundings?" I asked. "Surely they don't need to keep me here. After all, where would I escape to? They've got what they want."

"I'll try," he promised.

I thought it was about time I took a risk. If they weren't going to turn me loose without persuasion then it seemed a good idea to give Nathan a little leverage. I pulled him forward slightly, towards the corner of the cell remote from the door.

"Look," I said, loudly. "That's not good enough.

You have to *do* something about this. I don't want to hang about here for another week." Rapidly, and in a low whisper, I followed this statement with: "The code is in atomic numbers." The people outside couldn't have heard. But Nathan understood.

He nodded, and then looked down. We were standing very close to the big man's bunk, and his eyes—slightly bloodshot—were staring up at us. He'd heard, too.

"Be reasonable, Alex," said Nathan, clearly. "I know you haven't done anything. But Zarnecki thinks he has a strong case." Meanwhile, he directed a significant glance at the man on the bed, and raised an eyebrow.

He knows, I mouthed, without making any sound.

Nathan pursed his lips, but he nodded.

"Make Zarnecki show you the so-called evidence," I said. "Look it over very carefully. I think you'll find that it's pretty damn slim."

Privately, I didn't think there was much chance that Zarnecki would surrender the whole message. But it might be worth a try.

There wasn't much point in dragging out the fancy charade much further, and Nathan was about to put an end to the interview. But he didn't get a chance.

There was an almighty crash in the corridor outside, as of a heavy body being very firmly felled to the ground, and then the sound of struggling.

The door to the cell was wrenched open and Cade came in. He came in backwards, fighting for balance. He was trying desperately to draw the sword he wore at his belt, but he wasn't succeeding. He cannoned into Nathan and knocked him back against the wall, his left hand clutching for Nathan's clothing as he tried to support himself.

I was frozen stiff with astonishment, but not so the man on the bunk. Pained with withdrawal symptoms or not he was up like a shot. He shoved me down on to the lower bunk of the pair and grabbed Cade with both hands, virtually plucking him from the floor as he spun him around. His fist sank into Cade's gut, and I heard the air explode from Cade's lungs in a strangled grunt.

Cade went down, and my erstwhile companion was out the door like a ferret down a rabbit hole. There were still sounds of commotion in the corridor and now there came the sound of a single gunshot.

My instinct should have been to drop down and play dead until it all went quiet, but I was betrayed by my own reflexes. It seemed that I had a wholly unnecessary interest in who might have been shot. I ran to the door. Nathan tried to restrain me, but he tripped over Cade's prostrate form and fell, swearing loudly.

There were people all over the corridor, jostling furiously. One of the *gendarmes* was already down and either dead or unconscious. The other had managed to draw his gun, but his wrist was firmly in the grip of two other men, who had forced the pistol way up into the air. The bullet that he'd fired had hit the ceiling, but there was another man reeling from the fight with blood on his fingers as he clutched his left forearm, and I judged that he'd caught the ricochet. The man with the nose joined his friends hustling the gunman, and between the three of them they sent him crashing back against the stone wall with such force that all the wind was knocked out of him. One of the assailants grabbed the gun, the other clasped his hands together and brought them down hard to the side of the *gendarme*'s neck. He folded up instantly.

In the meantime, the big man turned round and

142

jerked me from the doorway of the cell into the corridor. He kicked the door of the cell shut and shot one of the bolts home. Inside, someone began thumping on the door. It had to be Nathan, unless Cade was a man of supernal powers of recuperation.

"What the hell—?" I began.

"You're coming," said the big man. "We need you." He began dragging me toward the door. Both of his companions were now armed, having dispossessed the officers of the law. Having seen what had happened, I didn't think it politic to stand up for my rights. They were in a hurry and there seemed to be a strong possibility of provoking further violence. I let myself be dragged.

Outside, the daylight seemed uncommonly bright. I blinked, and tried to shield my eyes, but I was still being hustled along. A third *gendarme* was propped against the outer wall of the building. He'd been laid out neatly, having presumably been slugged while he wasn't watching. There were several horses, milling around. They didn't know or approve of what was going on either.

Apparently, they'd only brought one spare mount, because my ex-cellmate cursed as he tried to push me up into a saddle and them climb up behind me. It was a complex operation, made no easier by the fact that I wasn't participating wholeheartedly. The others were on their horses and ready to go while he was still threatening me through gritted teeth. Somehow, I managed an appropriate amount of co-operation, and we both ended up on the animal's back. It wasn't comfortable for any of us, but I was probably suffering least, to judge by the horse's protests and the sweat that was pouring off the man behind me. At this proximity I could feel tremors in his body, and as he reached round me to manipulate the reins I could

143

see the unsteadiness and lack of real strength in his grip.

I knew he wasn't going to make it.

So, perhaps, did he. But he was going to have a damned good try. He was a tough man.

All the horses clattered off down the road, heading inland. There was no immediate indication of pursuit, but I knew that if we didn't get where we were going in one hell of a hurry there'd be an operation mounted that would make the hunting party of the previous night seem like a very small affair. I didn't know where we were going—whether they had a hiding place lined up or whether we were going to try and reach a boat waiting at some convenient spot—but there wasn't a second to be wasted in getting there.

Our horse, being by far the most inconvenienced in terms of load, and by no means the most strongly handled in that the man behind me was getting sicker by the minute, was soon last in the race and falling further behind with every stride. By the time we hit the woods on the east side of the township the others were forty or fifty yards ahead.

I'd had enough of being hustled. I didn't like it. And in view of the circumstances I didn't feel much compunction about hitting a sick man. I twisted sideways slightly to make room, and then with all the force I could muster I drove my right elbow backwards into his midriff. Then I knocked away one of his prisoning arms and jumped.

The horse had had enough of the terrible things that were being done to it. It shied, letting out a whinny that was almost a scream.

It spilled us both from its back, but the big man went down like a sack of potatoes, and when he hit the ground flat on his back I could see that I didn't have to worry about his getting angry with me. I rolled as I hit the ground, having expected to take a

144

tumble anyhow, and came out of it quite well. I was jarred, but I came quickly enough to my feet. Then I had to dive away again as the horse wheeled. There seemed to be flying hooves all over the place, mostly aimed at me. I sprawled in a bush.

Up ahead, they'd heard the horse's scream and looked back. They were reining in, and I knew I hadn't got much time. I made an inglorious exit from the far side of the bush and put the finishing touches to my resignation from the revolutionary cause by sprinting like hell for the cover of the trees.

If they'd been in the mood they could have ridden me down, but they had other things on their minds—their leader was stricken and his mount was in a state of high panic. Those were the problems which took priority. They didn't try to come after me. I zig-zagged through the woods for a half mile or so, until I was virtually certain that I couldn't be found even if they belatedly changed their minds. Then, feeling in desperate need of somewhere to hide out for a while and think things out, I climbed a tree whose branches sprawled close to the ground, and esconced myself in its crown, out of sight and perfectly safe.

15

For the first few minutes I didn't do anything except sag. My heart seemed to be going so fast that it was ringing rather than beating, like a demented alarm clock. My legs ached and I kept discovering bruises. My right arm, never fully recovered from the injuries sustained on Dendra, was reminding me that it shouldn't be asked to do too much. But I was still in good working order, and in time I felt a great deal better.

I tried to weigh up the new situation.

Poseidon's answer to Robin Hood had tried to snatch me so that I could decode his thrice bedamned secret message for him. Unfortunately, the only one of the witnesses who could actually testify that I'd been taken along against my will was Nathan, and I didn't really give a lot for his chances of being believed. Which meant that if I'd been classed as an undesirable before I could well be public enemy number one by now. The big search operation wouldn't just be for the outlaws. They'd be after me, too.

The obvious course of action was to turn myself in. The revolution wasn't my problem . . . they could fight it without me. The sensible thing to do was probably to take the obvious course of action. We'd run our course on this world now, and it seemed wisest to accept the decisions of fate.

But there were two reasons why I didn't altogether fancy being sensible. Firstly, I didn't want to end up back in a cell waiting for everything to be tidied up. And secondly, I now had more than a hint about where whatever went on here that we weren't supposed to know about was to be found. I had developed a truly insatiable curiosity about whatever was lurking in the cellars of James Wildeblood's mansion. I was damned if I was going to let things take their course in a meek and mild fashion while I had any chance of getting to the bottom of things.

And so I tried to weigh up my chances.

They didn't look bad. Getting to the house would be risky, but maybe it would be the last place they'd expect me to go. In all likelihood the dogs would be out working instead of patrolling the grounds. The window in the west wing was almost certainly still open—discreetly wedged by the pebble I'd put in to secure my means of re-entry the previous night. And once in the deserted west wing I shouldn't meet any interference in locating a cellar in the north-west corner.

Once there, the next step might be obvious or undiscoverable. But the way to find out was to go.

By night, naturally.

The hours to nightfall didn't seem such a bad prospect. Stuck up a tree seemed to be no less attractive than being stuck in a stone cage. The trouble was, however, that there were still a great many hours to go until darkness came again, and the branches of the tree were even less comfortable than the hard straw mattress on the bunk. What was more, if I'd been in the cell I would probably have been fed. There didn't seem to be any prospect of finding a square meal anywhere in the woods.

After an hour or so, I began to doubt the wisdom of my decision in no uncertain terms. But I knew that I'd never make it back to the ship, which was one place they *would* be expecting me to go, and my pride kept getting in the way of serious contemplation of the other credible alternative—surrender.

So I stayed put. Now and again, I got down to stretch my legs and look around. I changed trees twice for a bit of variety. I contemplated the local wonders of nature, watching the insects and the worms.

I kept my ears constantly at work listening for the sound of anyone else in the wood. I was afraid that I might have to hide from a dragnet, and I was even more afraid that if they had the dogs out I might not manage it. To be caught up a tree would undoubtedly be even more ignominious than being forced to give myself up.

But this particular fear proved to be unfounded. I could only conjecture that the search was being concentrated in another area. Probably, the fleeing riders had been sighted some way from here and had drawn the search after them. It was, after all, a big island, and last night's operation had only covered the ground in the locale of the house. Given enough time and horses with enough strength, the rebels could have been thirty miles or more away by noon.

It was a long and tedious day, but it passed at last, and as soon as the twilight grew grey I began making my way toward the great house. I went with all due care and in no particular hurry, glad at last to be doing something positive. It got too dark a little too quickly for my liking, but it was another clear night, and I found myself a solid staff of wood about as long as I was tall, and used that to help me pick my way through the tangles of vegetation. I seemed to make a terrible amount of noise, rustling and rattling my way through thickets and patches of fern—Poseidon's woods were preternaturally quiet places, without the whistles and croaks and multitudinous whispers that characterize most woodlands—but nobody was there to hear me.

I found the road, eventually, and moved like a shadow along it, until I came to the iron rail that bounded the Wildeblood private estate. It took only a couple of minutes to scale the barrier, and then I ran quickly for the shelter of the coppices of trees that bounded the lawns. After my experience of the night before I decided to risk the open lawns rather than the more inviting but treacherous cover of the rear of the house. I crouched as low as I could while I moved smoothly and quickly across the vast open space to the shadowy walls, and made it unchallenged and unobserved.

I made my way slowly round the inner quadrangle of the house, treading very carefully indeed as I passed by the great doors, and ultimately found the west wing and the window I had conveniently secured as a means of access.

Hastily, I clambered in, and eased the window shut behind me, slipping the pebble into my pocket. I fumbled along the wall for a candlebracket, and found one. I took out the candles, and then repeated the procedure, until I had a collection of eight. What I didn't have was a match, but I kept on checking the brackets, sure that there would be a light somewhere. On a small shelf beneath the candleholder nearest to the door I found half a dozen, together with sanded paper on which they could be struck and some tapers. I took the matches and the paper, and didn't bother with the tapers.

I had to take the risk of lighting a candle and carrying it with me. I couldn't fumble my way through the corridors as I had the previous night. Then, I had known where I was going. This time, I didn't. I couldn't find my way through the maze by touch. If the light were seen as I passed a window, and the person who saw it thought anything of it, that would be too bad.

But, with the candle lighted, it didn't take me long to find a set of stone steps leading down from the ground floor to the subterranean part of the house. I went swiftly down, away from windows and the danger of curious eyes, feeling a little more confident.

I hadn't seen a great deal of the house above ground. We had always been discouraged from exploratory wandering. Of its layout below ground I knew nothing at all. I had no way of guessing how extensive the network of cellars and passages might be. The discovery of the word "celare" in the message had not surprised me, and had, in fact, seemed possessed of a certain propriety. It is the sort of thing one expects to find in a cryptogram, once decoded.

But when I reached the bottom of the flight of steps I realized that the cellars of Wildeblood's mansion were not to be taken for granted.

I found myself in a corridor which extended in two directions, but ran only twelve or fifteen feet either way before bending away at right-angles. There were no doors in the corridor. I took the direction which most closely approximated to north-west. But no sooner had I taken the bent (which pointed me towards the south-west) than I found a junction. I took the arm which headed west. Ten feet further on there was another junction, this time presenting three alternatives. I had still not found a door set in the corridor wall.

There was only one possible conclusion. Underneath his house—this part of it, at least—James Wildeblood had constructed a labyrinth. It was just too much. In one sense, it was worrying ... but in another, it was bordering on the comical. I took one of the corridors at random, and moved along it, barely suppressing an urge to laugh out loud.

But then I discovered that it wasn't funny.

I still had the long stick I'd picked up to assist me in the wood. I'd been carrying it ever since simply because I hadn't found much of a reason to relinquish it. I'd mounted the candle in a tray that I could carry in my left hand, and had put the rest of the paraphernalia in my pocket. The stick I was carrying in my right hand, slanted from the horizontal so that its front end scraped along the floor. I was doing this almost automatically, with no particular purpose in mind.

And then suddenly, the end was no longer supported and the stick twisted in my hand. Had I let go, it would have slid away over the edge of a hole to whose very edge my feet had brought me.

I stopped dead, and slowly crouched, bringing the candle down. The gaping hole extended all the way across the corridor—and, in fact, it seemed that the passage had been made narrower here so as to accommodate exactly the proportions of the trap.

I fumbled in my pocket, and found the pebble I'd used to jam the window. I dropped it into the hole.

And waited out a long, long silence that ended with a tiny, very distant splash.

If I'd counted the seconds I could have worked a quick equation to find out how far down it was. But I hadn't, and it didn't really matter. It was far enough. One more step would have been the fatal one.

"You bastard," I muttered, addressing the ghost of James Wildeblood. "You could have mentioned it."

Perhaps he had, of course. I only had the first few words of the message.

I worked my way back to the junction, and took

151

the next best alternative. This time I went very carefully indeed, using the stick to probe the floor before me.

But the next thing that disappeared wasn't the floor—it was one of the walls. Suddenly, I was no longer in a tunnel of brick and mortar but one of natural rock, whose walls opened rapidly into an uneven chamber. The floor of the chamber had been worked with tools—as it was gathered up into a blind alley a narrow cranny in the floor had been widened, and steps were cut into its slanting side. This semi-natural staircase looked both narrow and steep. It was about ten inches across—enough to take me if I stood sideways, but not enough to allow me to turn. I'd have to go down like a crab, trying to look over my shoulder all the while to check the depth of the next step. A fat man would not have been able to get down it at all, and I wasn't sure that it was a particularly inviting prospect so far as I was concerned.

But something told me that this was it. You don't cut steps in a narrow slit through faces of cold rock unless you have a very good reason for doing so. Building a corridor to lead to a pitfall was relatively easy, if you had the nasty mind to want it done. But this wasn't just an invitation to disaster. Much pain and effort had gone into preparing this way.

Carefully, left arm and candle leading, I eased myself into the crack. I couldn't get the end of the staff past me to test the steps, so I held the candle as low as was practicable and did a balancing act on each ledge while I sought the next with the toe of my boot. It wasn't a nice way to travel, but it got me down . . . and down. . . .

It was obvious now that Wildeblood had built his house over the entrance to a natural system of caves. Such systems were common enough on Wildeblood, thanks to the geological peculiarities of the upper rock-strata. This one, to judge by the splash at the bottom of the sucker-drop, extended all the way down to sea level and was connected by deep passages to the ocean.

If I wanted to hide something, it was just the kind of place I'd pick. Heaven only knew how many other nasty surprises there were waiting for wanderers in the labyrinth, and maybe the staircase I'd picked, guided in my decision by the message, was the only one which gave you even a sporting chance of getting to the proper entrance intact.

There had been no mention of any such considerable cave system on this island in James Wildeblood's survey report. And yet he must have found it while he was a member of that team. What, I wondered, had he found *in* it that had made him keep quiet about it? Or had it been merely one more piece in a jigsaw-puzzle plan that would end with his owning a world?

I reached the bottom of the rock staircase. Here the cleft widened again, and there was a triangular apron of rock about seven feet from the apex, where I stood, to the base, which was a ledge.

Cautiously, I moved forward to the edge, and knelt down. I could feel the coldness of the stone through my trouser legs. I peered over the lip of the ledge, but could see no bottom in the Stygian darkness. All that I did find was a pair of steel pegs driven deep into the rim and plugged with some kind of cement. Dangling from the pegs was a rope ladder, doubled up so that the bottom was looped around the top rung. The rope was tough—and new. By no stretch of the imagination had it been hanging there since James Wildeblood's pioneer explorations. This route into the underworld was still in use.

I unhooked the bottom of the ladder from the

top and let it fall away into the abyss. Why, I wondered, was it secured thus instead of simply left dangling? The answer that immediately occurred to me wasn't one I liked much.

There is no way that a man can safely descend a rope ladder clutching a candle-tray in one hand and a quarterstaff in the other. So the staff had to go. I left it on the ledge, and gingerly eased myself over the rim of the pit, clutching one of the pegs in my left hand and holding the candle in my right. I could have put out the candle and used both arms but that would have left me to go down in total darkness, and there was no way I could face the terrible prospect of getting to the bottom and then finding that I couldn't light a match. I hadn't all that much faith in the matches, which—unlike the rope of the ladder—hadn't been recently renewed.

The first few rungs were bad, while I extended myself fully on the ladder. Then I could find some kind of a rhythmic procedure, lowering the grip of each limb in turn. I thought it would be easier all the way to the bottom, but I had reckoned without the architecture of this particular cavern. Only the first ten or twelve feet of the ladder lay against the face of the rock, which was slanted from the vertical by four or five degrees in my favor. After that the slant changed and the remainder of the ladder hung absolutely plumb as the nearby wall retreated into the gloom.

I was becalmed in a limitless void of black, clammy emptiness, in which only the twin ropes and the frail wooden spars connecting them had any meaningful existence. All that prevented me from falling into what might—so far as I could know—be a bottomless abyss was a foothold and the deathlike grip of my left hand. Every time I had to move that hand I wrapped my right arm round the rope, deliberately tangling myself in case a foot should slip. And every time I executed that complex winding manoeuver, the candle guttered. . . .

I tried telling myself how lucky I was that I had a candle instead of a flashlight. The candle would warn me of foul air, by going out . . .

Somehow, I didn't manage to reassure myself.

It quickly became agonizing for me to reach down with the leading foot, to unlock my hand or arm. The pain was not physical but psychological, and no less painful for that. I cursed myself for idly unlooping the bottom of the ladder and letting it fall, without hauling the whole thing up to count the rungs. And I cursed James Wildeblood for his vicious secrets. I no longer wondered at the fact that no one had ever penetrated his clandestine operations. If this were the only route, then the wonder was that Philip was actually afraid that someone *might* discover it. We all know that familiarity breeds contempt, but if Philip and Zarnecki were so familiar with this procedure that they could nip up and down the near-vertical corridor twice a week then they had my profoundest admiration. It seemed to me while I descended that ladder that I had found a species of hell.

And then came the moment of utter horror, when I reached for another rung and found that it wasn't there. I groped with the toe of my boot for *something* where the rung ought to have been—five or six inches beneath the last, but found nothing. A little higher I discovered the dangling loop of rope. The ladder was finished. Logically, I could drop safely to the ground.

But who trusts logic in such a situation? I remembered the pitfall, and the rope-ladder suddenly seemed to me nothing more than more sophisticated kind of trap—a lure, inviting the curious to a nasty-minded doom. It dawned on my frightened mind that this was probably the whole intention of Wildeblood's coded message: it was all bait to bring fools into a labyrinth from which there was no conceivable release. The whole thing had been the cruellest of cruel jokes. . . .

How far dared I reach with my trailing foot?

I wanted to let go and jump. I wanted desperately to be able to persuade myself to let go and jump. But my fears just would not find the arguments convincing, and I couldn't blame them. Trust in terror, I thought, because it is the most faithful of all our guardians.

My hand, which had seemed for so many moments to have a miraculous capacity to freeze itself to the rope, lock on with a superhuman tenacity, gradually began to slip.

Fearfully, I wound my right arm around again, and let my left hand down. My searching foot descended a few inches more. There was nothing. I had to repeat the whole sequence, letting it down again, feeling all the while that the floor *must* be there, and if it was not, then . . .

My boot touched the bottom.

It was there. Cold stone.

I would not immediately trust it. I tested it with my legs as far as I could stretch myself . . . testing firmness and extent. I could not accept its solidity without suspicion and confirmation.

But rock it was, and an expanse of rock quite large enough for any human purpose.

I let myself down to it, and let the faint light of the candle illuminate it for me. There was a wall curving away into darkness, and a crevice. There were water marks there—sinuous colored curves etched into the face. It was damp, but there was no trace of running water now. I followed the wall, intending to stick close by it. I didn't want to wander off into some vast pitted amphitheatre. I held the candle up high, to follow the track left by the water, and then caught my breath.

I can't describe now the feelings which overwhelmed me then as I saw what I saw. There was anger, disgust, a terrible sense of my own stupidity. Up there was an electric cable. And dangling from it, secured in a cage of wire mesh, was an electric bulb. Without doubt the whole dangerous way was discreetly wired. When generators had been built to supply the house they had not neglected its most vital extension. Of course not.

If only, back on that triangular ledge, I had held my candle *up* to the ceiling, instead of *down* to reach into the perilous darkness, I would probably have seen the switch.

Mentally, I cancelled the admiration I'd found for Zarnecki and Philip. They didn't deserve it. The way I had come ceased to be anywhere near as frightening once I realized that it could be lighted.

On the other hand, I remembered, when James Wildeblood had first come this way there had been no steep spikes supporting a rope ladder, no steps cut into that narrow slit.

I continued to follow, not the wall, but the cable. It had to be going where I wanted to go.

There was still a slope to the tunnel, which carried me downwards still. Out of the darkness another wall loomed, drawing in on me. I wondered, briefly, what might have happened had I followed the *other* wall—the one without the cable. I felt relief that I had, in fact, seen the thing when I did.

I passed through a globular grotto with three modes of egress, but had no difficulty selecting my way. I had to crouch at one point, and several times I had to be careful lest I slip on the damp stone, which was pitted with rivulets where water habitually ran. I prayed that it would not start to rain heavily up above.

But then the runnel arced away into a drain set beside the path, and finally disappeared into a yawning hole while the passage flattened out somewhat.

And twenty feet or so into this dry, horizontal passage I found a brick wall, into which was set a heavy wooden door, reinforced by iron strips. The door must have been assembled here long, long ago ... and the bricks let down in panniers, with mortar and tools.

That was a lot of trouble to go to for no particular reason. I knew I'd reached my destination. I inspected the door closely. It had a lock, but the key hanging on a nail driven into the wood close to it. There was also a single heavy bolt, centrally placed and presently closed.

All of this perturbed me somewhat. I remembered the rope ladder, drawn up and looped to the supports. Now a lock with a key on a nail, and a bolt shot home on *this* side of the door. All three of these were precautions ... not for the purpose of keeping unwelcome visitors and trespassers out, but for the purpose of keeping someone—or something—very definitely *in*.

16

Slowly, and as quietly as was humanly possible, I drew back the bolt. Then I turned the key in the lock. It wasn't stiff.

The door opened toward me, and at first I opened it only a crack in order to peer around it. But I could see nothing—it was pitch dark on the other side except for a mere line of light that seemed to be very distant. I pulled it wide open and went through, candle held high.

It was something of an anti-climax.

I was in a closed section of tunnel—a kind of ante-room. The apparent great distance of the line of light had been an optical illusion caused by the lack of reference points. It was, in fact, shining under another door that was only four or five paces away. The closed section was filled with sacks and barrels, piled on either side with only a narrow corridor running between them.

One of the barrels was open, and I checked its contents. It contained a coarse substance, grey-green in color, with something of the texture of sand. It was like soft gravel to the touch. It was dried plankton.

Is this, I wondered, the source of the drug? It seemed too simple.

I looked for another empty container, and located a second topless barrel. But this one contained cabbages. I also located a sackful of turnips.

We were now a long way underground, but it wasn't as cold as I might have expected. It was rather more than a couple of degrees above freezing, but probably cold enough for this food to keep some time without spoiling. But what was it for?

The other door hadn't a lock or a bolt. I only had to pull the handle to draw it open.

And this time, when I peered through the thin crack, it wasn't into darkness that I looked, but into the dull illumination of low-efficiency electric lights. They were not near enough or bright enough to dazzle, and they were not adequate to show every corner of the great vaulted chamber where they hung. They sat among stalactites, throwing startling shadows that made the roof of the cave into an amazing forest of glowing stone daggers and criss-crossing black stripes.

The cave was enormous . . . as large in capacity as the hall wherein James Wildeblood had gathered the relics of his collection of Poseidoniana. The ceiling formed a great dome, pocketed here and there but basically hemispherical. The floor was also concave, like a bowl, with three ledges let into it and a sector cut out at the lowest level which was filled with water. There was a flat black slit extending about twenty degrees of arc—nearly fifty feet—at the far side of the cave where the water extended its surface out of the chamber and into what must be a whole system of natural sewers and conduits. Here were the sea caves of Wildeblood's island, a network extending over a hundred square miles, in all likelihood. How much of it was accessible from here was anyone's guess. One thing I was sure of, though, was that its connections with the sea were all underwater. For all practical human purposes, this had to be the only way in.

As I looked around the great dome, I saw other tunnels and slits—perhaps a dozen in all—let into this central pocket. Some of them, at least, would be the highways of this inner world. Secured to the concave ledge at the water's edge were three small wooden boats, draped with assorted net and tackle. The waterways, too, were navigable thoroughfares.

Beside me, on the platform which allowed access to the door, were small boxes filled with bags—each bag about the size of a fist. Spilled here or smeared there were traces of a white powder I didn't need to taste in order to identify.

On the second level, below the platform, there was a positive maze of apparatus—iron and glass, like the laboratory of an alchemist as imagined by a Gothic writer of long ago. It was bizarre and makeshift, but as I looked at it I could see beyond the superficial ludicrous abundance of tubes and clamps to the reality of its functioning. Almost at a glance, I understood. It was a processing plant, for dehydration, separation, distillation. This great vault was warmer than it had any right to be, so far down in the bowels of the island. The reason now was clear—strategically arranged beneath the device was a system of coils for electrical heating.

This was where the drug was made, all right.

But I didn't immediately wonder about its source, because there was something else which caught and held my attention absolutely, forming within me a slow, cold core of horror and realization.

I saw the people who made it.

Working the apparatus were three men—or, to be strictly accurate, three human beings, for two were female. They might have been any age between fifteen and fifty. I couldn't tell. I couldn't tell because their hair was white, their faces were white, their flesh was tight around their skullbones. They were dressed in grey tunics and trousers, not ragged but old.

They didn't even look up.

I pulled back the door until it bumped on the

sack of turnips, and pushed myself through it to stand on the platform of stone, looking down at them. They knew I was there, but they just went on with what they were doing, refusing to look at me or acknowledge my existence. They worked on steadily and patiently, as if there were nothing else in the universe but their perennial task.

Secrets that people are particularly anxious to keep, I thought, are often nastier than you imagine.

I had known that Philip's secret would be the making of the drug. But I hadn't sat down to work out all the implications. A secret place, that had to be kept secret. Had I imagined that Philip and Zarnecki did the work with their own fair hands? Or that Elkanah and the other servants worked by day in the house and by night on their secret project? I'd known, in my mind, that the production of enough drug to supply a colony wasn't a back yard operation. It needed people, supplies, power. But it had never occurred to me that Wildeblood had a little colony within a colony . . . slaves, toiling away in a little private underworld . . . or private hell.

There had to be more than three. Thirty, maybe . . . or even more. The rest were elsewhere in the world of tunnels—living, working. The whole operation was down here. It had to be. Everything, from the harvest to the product. Whatever the source of the drug was, it had to be down here in the caves and canals. The whole life of this little prisoner community, with skins dead white because they had never been exposed to the sun, was given over to the production of the power and the wealth of the Wildeblood dynasty.

I jumped down from the platform of stone, and moved toward the three people silently tendering their monstrous machine. I touched the man on the shoulder, and he turned to look at me. There was an expression in his eyes of infinite patience. The eyes had once been brown—or had been intended by his genes to be brown. Now they were orange, with a hint of green, faded toward the pink of albinism but not quite getting there. They were bright eyes.

"Can you talk?" I said. It was an idiotic question. Why should they be dumb?

"Yes," he said. He showed no surprise at the question.

He saw me. He wasn't blind. The electric lights were enough to preserve his sight. He stared into my face, uncaring, waiting. I dropped my hand, and let him turn back. Unasked was the question: How long have you been here?

I already knew the answer.

All my life.

All of countless lives. No one ever left here. Perhaps new blood was periodically introduced, to supplement the birth rate. But they would be brought as children, to grow accustomed to the life and to know of nothing else.

I searched for other questions, but I had lost them all. I just couldn't speak.

I walked toward the water's edge, toward the boats. But then something did remind itself to me, and I turned aside. I went to the hoppers that stood at one end of the apparatus—the end where the raw material had to be put in. I looked inside the barrels which held the supply, ready for the distillation to begin.

And I saw a translucent gel, organized into thick branching strands, moist and limp. Within the gel were embedded thousands of black dots, each one the size of a thumbnail but perfectly round.

There was no mistaking it.

It was spawn. The spawn of the whaleys, deposited here in underground caves, in the dark

163

world where the seafaring predators would not go. A small measure of parental care . . . eggs laid where they would be as safe as it was possible to make them.

But safe no longer. After millions of years of evolution, chance had thrown up a century of Wildeblood's empire. A new kind of depredation. I knew then what the boats and nets were for, and where the rest of the white people must be.

The breeding season had begun. They were gathering in the harvest.

The gel was provided not merely as a matrix for the embryos but also as their initial food supply. Millions of tiny hatchlings would live the first weeks of their lives here, growing a little before their vast migration back across the ocean bed to join the herds in the open sea. By nature's calculation one in ten thousand might survive to reach the herd. The rest would provide food for the many hunters of the inshore waters. That, at least, had been the plan.

Wildeblood had introduced an ecological short-circuit. Now, the slaughter took place at a much earlier stage, before the hatching. The survival rate of those whaleys which were allowed to hatch was cut, but the *real* sufferers—the immediate sufferers—would be the fish and the invertebrate carnivores.

We had taken samples of sea water, analyzed the population of the plankton. I hadn't had time yet to compare our findings in any great detail against the population of the sea as recorded by the survey team. But I knew now what we would find.

An ecological catastrophe. Sweeping changes, which had begun in a small way over a hundred years ago but which were now in the process of exponential increase. Whole food chains interrupted, at first on a small scale, but by now on a vast one. Thousands of species threatened with extinction, at least locally.

Including—and perhaps most significantly of all —the whaleys.

We'd had so little time to attempt so much. We were short-handed because both Conrad and Linda had gone with Mariel. Single-handed, I might not have detected this until we were in hyperspace, expelled from the planet for imagined crimes concocted in service of the great secret. Philip didn't want us to know about his underworld full of slaves. Of the wider implications, he had no idea.

I knew then why James Wildeblood had taken the apparently-ludicrous move of leaving behind a message. I knew now what it said, in the later part that I'd never seen. He'd known that his empire was mortal . . . temporary. Its decline and fall was ecologically predestined.

The message was an appeal for help. Help from Earth. Help to save the colony which had developed handsomely in embryo but which *must*— now or someday—go through the extremely painful process of birth into another kind of reliance upon its own resources and those of the world. James Wildeblood had hoped—and perhaps it was a desperate hope, because there was no way of knowing now what kind of contact with Earth he had envisaged—that there might be a midwife to assist in the process.

I could see it all now. I realized that without James Wildeblood's message, I would never have been able to figure it out. I would have discovered the changes that were happening in the sea, but I wouldn't have known why. I wouldn't have been able to figure out just what was happening. Not in a month, or a year.

What kind of a man, I wondered again, was Wildeblood?

I shook my head, because I just didn't know. I couldn't understand him.

And then a voice behind me, soft and sibilant, spoke my name.

17

Wrapped up in my dreadful imagination, I had not heard their footfalls. They had come through the doors I had left open without needing to move them. They had come quietly, treading softly.

They were only two. They hadn't brought a posse. Naturally not. Just Zarnecki and Cade. All in the family.

Zarnecki held a naked sword, the point directed at my throat. Cade had a gun—a large calibre revolver like the ones that *gendarmes* carried. That was pointed in my direction too.

"How did you know I was here?" I asked.

Zarnecki smiled. "Your friend told Philip this evening that he knew the key to the code. That puzzled me. It seemed to me that if he'd had it before he would have tried to bargain with it before. It occurred to me that perhaps he'd only recently found out. You told him, Mr. Alexander ... in the cell, this morning. Cade heard you whisper but he didn't know what. I was worried. I'm a very cautious man. I left Philip and your confederate arguing, and came down ... just to make sure that all was well. Then I found that someone had let down the rope ladder, and left a wooden pole on the ledge.

"We've been out hunting for you all day, Mr. Alexander. We caught your friend the musician, although some of *his* friends managed to elude us. We'll have them all, in due course. We couldn't imagine where you'd got to; we felt sure that you'd head for the ship. But we didn't suspect then that you might know the way down here."

I stared at the blade of the sword, feeling helpless. The breath that was caught up in my throat eased past my vocal cords, but I couldn't find words. I didn't know what to say.

Zarnecki was having no difficulty, though.

"Now you know everything," he said. "Don't you?"

I swallowed air, then let my pent-up breath go in a deep sigh. I found my body relaxing, letting itself fall back into readiness.

I found my voice.

"Everything," I said. "Perhaps more than you do."

I spoke normally, but the echoes took what I said and stirred it slightly, rippling the remnants round the circular chamber in an eerie residual whisper.

"I even know why you tipped your hand by giving us the second copy of the code," I said, slowly. "You're in trouble. The operation has reached its limit. The colony is expanding and by over-exploitation you're shrinking the population of the whaleys. This season, you're at or near to the crossover point, and after that there's only disaster. You thought—just as the musician did—that the code might hold the secret of an alternative source of supply. You hoped we might give you the key without being able to deduce too much from the initial fragment. You were no cleverer than the big man, your reasoning was almost exactly the same. But you were both wrong."

"That remains to be seen," said Zarnecki, "when your friend deciphers the message for us."

"Don't be a fool, Zarnecki," I said. "There isn't an alternative. You must know that. There are other islands, other caves. But to gain *access* to another system the way you have here is something else again. And even if there *is* such a thing, who's going to find it for you? Who's going to work it? How are you going to keep your secret then? This place is useful to you because you're sitting right on top of it. Another source on another island splits your power base in two. And that doesn't just make you twice as vulnerable, it makes an eventual division and argument inevitable. And what happens when you need a third source, and a fourth...? You're finished, Zarnecki. You and Philip and the family. This season, or next, or the one after. Your time is up."

"So is yours, Mr. Alexander," he said, in a tone which could only be described as pregnant with menace.

"What do you hope to gain?" I asked. "Even if you keep your secret, it's no good to you. You can't keep supplying the whole colony; there isn't enough..."

I trailed off. I saw, suddenly, why they wanted rid of us now. They didn't want us to stay out the summer. They didn't want us to see how they intended to handle their problem. We had come to make a report on them, to carry back to Earth ... and they were ready to let us do that, so long as they could show in a favorable light. But they didn't want to take the risk of our reporting back to Earth the kind of measures they intended to take when the drug that kept their tyranny moderately benevolent ran out ...

They already had the political apparatus of power. When they could no longer hold it by euphoric persuasion they intended to hold it by force and firepower. They were expecting riots just as soon as the addicts were told that the supply was being withheld. Riots and bloodshed. They didn't want us around when the lid came off. They

169

wanted to have their war in private . . . like their little underworld colony of slaves.

And then I knew that Zarnecki intended to kill me. Exile was no longer enough. He wouldn't face the thought that the whole thing was out of the bag, ready to be relayed back to Earth. And why not? Primarily, because of his pride. His honor. The system of personal protection that, on a world like this one, meant so much.

My eyes were held by the point of the sword. I expected it to run me through at any moment.

But I was wrong.

Absurdly—but quite logically—I was wrong.

Zarnecki handed the sword to Cade, who accepted it. Then, from a sheath in Cade's belt, he took a knife. It had a blade some five inches long, with one sharp edge and a point made by the convergence of a concave curve on the sharp edge and a convex one on the blunt side. From his own belt he took a similar knife—not quite identical but near enough. He flipped this one over in his hand after showing it to me, and offered it, hilt first.

He couldn't just cut me down. He had to do it by the book. He hadn't brought his duelling kit with him, so the knives would have to do.

I almost felt like laughing. But it was serious. Like everything else on this crazy world, it wasn't a joke. All he had to do was let Cade shoot me dead. But in a very real sense he *couldn't*. That was what it was all about, in the final analysis. Preserving the image. Keeping up appearances. A matter of pride.

They would kill us for *that*. In the ritual manner.

I was being offered a chance that no reasonable, ruthless man would have offered. But even so, I could hardly feel confident. In a knife fight, or in any kind of a fight to the death, he had all the advantages except one. He was still a fraction slower, thanks to the drug.

Unlike Nathan, though, I wouldn't be artificially speeded up. And I didn't know the moves. I contemplated refusing to fight . . . the neo-Christian way. I'd tried it once before, and it had worked. But only by courtesy of an accident. I'd misjudged my man. There could be no misjudging Zarnecki. If I refused to fight he'd feel morally justified in butchering me.

I took the knife.

He didn't just dive in. He took up a sort of crouch, a posture that ritualistically signalled his readiness to begin. He waited for me to do likewise. I looked at him. He'd placed his feet widely apart, and he was leaning slightly forward, his arms wide.

Not being a complete idiot, I didn't copy him. Instead, I aimed a sudden vicious kick at his crotch.

But he wasn't a complete idiot, either. He'd never been convinced that I knew how to act like a gentleman and he wasn't fool enough to take it for granted that I would. He was ready for me.

He caught my flying boot in his left hand and ever-so-gently redirected its course, pushing it sideways and getting the heel of his hand underneath it. Then he jerked upwards. Without using much force he hurled me over on my back, and I went down like a ton of bricks.

The rock was very, very hard, and the impact jarred my whole body, sending spears of pain up my back and paralyzing my right arm. Luckily, I had accepted the knife into my left because of the stiffness already inherent in the right.

If he'd been content to maim me he could have slashed the muscles of my leg and made sure of eventual victory, but he was still fighting by his rules and he wanted a clean kill.

As he came after me I used my legs again, this time to trap his ankle and trip him. Somehow, I managed it. He went down too, but only to his knees. Nevertheless, I was up first, and backing away before he was ready again. He came after me, carefully, still in his crouch. I continued to retreat, uneasily. When he lunged, bringing his arm across in a great horizontal arc, I didn't dare try to catch his wrist. I just jumped back out of the way. I had to keep dodging, use my quickness. If it came to a straightforward contest of strength he'd probably win.

He came on again, with another sweeping flourish of the blade. It seemed silly, because it was such a wide, slow arc that it was easy to avoid it.

Far too easy.

I jumped back, and suddenly there wasn't anything to jump back to. My eyes and my mind had been entirely bound up with watching the blade. I'd forgotten where I was. And I'd reached the second ledge. I fell heavily about three feet, twisting my ankle slightly and falling. I rolled over and over, trying to get out of reach as he came down after me, and rolled off the shelf of rock into the water.

It was icy cold. As my whole body was immersed the cold stabbed into my flesh with a single convulsive squeeze which nearly took the life out of me. I shut my eyes and my mouth, and tried to curl up as I fell through the water. Somehow, I couldn't make my legs kick, I couldn't begin to swim.

I just went down and down, until I touched bottom . . .

Only it wasn't bottom.

It was cold and it was smooth, but it wasn't rock. It was skin. The skin of an amphibian.

How I managed to react so fast, I don't know.

The shock of the cold water had immobilized me, perhaps the second shock simply switched me back on again. But however chance or nature served me, I took full advantage. I twisted in the water, let my feet touch the great expanse of flesh, and thrust upwards, straightening like an arrow as my hands reached out for the surface. Somehow, I had lost the knife, but I didn't care. There was only one idea in my whole mind and that was the knowledge that I didn't want to play games in a deep, dark pool with a beast the size of a small whale.

My eyes opened, and I saw the surface above as a shimmer of gold, roiled and rippled by countless curved shadows. I saw it only for a second before I burst through it, my hands already groping towards the sharp horizon of rock which bordered it.

I gripped the shelf, my head burst from the water, and I saw the black shadow of Zarnecki reaching down for me. This time there was no conceivable option. As the blade carved the air, heading for my neck, I grabbed the wrist and pulled with all my might. I forced the blade up and past my ear, and continued the pull.

He was already off balance making the lunge. He toppled right over me and into the water, water that was already beginning to bubble and swell. The coldness had the same effect on him as it had had on me. He went straight under.

Grabbing the shelf with both hands, and feeling the water surging beneath me, I hauled myself out with a single mighty effort of my whole frame. Once on the rock I rolled away from the edge with a panic-stricken urgency.

I turned in time to see the head of the whaley break surface. It seemed unbelievably large, the eyes like fiery pits burning yellow in the electric light, the size of soup plates. The skin was white, mottled on the upper part of green. The mouth never opened, but looked something like a gigantic turtle's beak, hard and curved.

And from a great long gash behind one eye, dark red blood was gushing.

On the way down, Zarnecki had met the monster coming up, and had slashed at it with all his might. To the sea-beast, it was but a pin-prick.... it was probably only alarm at the invasion of privacy that made the thing twist and turn so, making the water foam and bringing all parts of the creature's leviathan length into crushing contact with the rocky walls of its mighty cranny.

But as it thrashed and twisted and churned, and made the pool seem to boil despite its iciness ...

Nothing could survive in the water, then. Nothing.

Cade was forward and firing—firing at the monstrous head. He hit it, twice at least, though he fired four or five times more. More blood gouted out of two holes ripped in the soft flesh by the large-calibre bullets. The head dived again.

I knew the whaley wouldn't die. The bullets, though fired at point-blank range, wouldn't penetrate the thick skull.

I took my chance. I came to my feet, kicked Cade in the kidneys, and took the gun from him when he fell. I pointed it at him, threatening him with it although I knew that it was almost certainly empty.

But then came a voice ... yet *another* voice. This one hadn't counted the shots, and didn't appear to be much of a judge of character. What it said was:

"Alex! For God's sake don't shoot!"

Needless to say, I didn't.

18

Nathan and Philip were standing by the open door, on the tall platform. There were a couple of others behind them, standing back where I couldn't see them clearly. I recognized Elkanah by the bandage on his head.

Even in the cave itself the audience was growing. There were five of the frail, white ghosts now—two more had come from one of the tunnel mouths, attracted, no doubt, by the shooting.

I lobbed the useless revolver into the churning water. There was no sign of the amphibian now. I didn't think it would come back. Who could blame it? I didn't think Zarnecki would be back either. There was no sign of him.

"Well now," I said, with more than the hint of a sneer. "What's this—a conducted tour?"

"It's okay," said Nathan.

"Oh sure," I said. "You talked him round, right?"

He came down, and as he approached his eyes were full of warning.

"I told Philip that we had the key to the code."

"I know," I said, bitterly. "And that sent Zarnecki down here just to make sure. And when he found me ..."

"He should have stayed a little longer," said Nathan. "I pointed out to Philip that the secret was out, now. I knew ... you knew ... Conrad knew ... the man in the cell with you knew ... and all his friends."

175

I knew better than to raise an eyebrow at the slightly-stretched truth.

"I offered Philip our help," said Nathan. "All the help we can give him. I told him that whatever he was facing, we could help him solve it. I made him see that there wasn't any point in getting rid of us, not any more. When I told him that you already knew what was in the message because of the copy Zarnecki had given us ... he agreed to tell me the whole thing."

His eyes still said that I'd better be careful, that I mustn't take the risk of blowing the whole operation by confessing that only I—and now he—really knew any more than the barest elements of the story. And they also said that I had to go along with him.

"We've made a deal, have we?" I said, my voice low and acid. I knew that Philip could hear me, but I didn't care. "You're going to save all this for Philip." I indicated by a gesture that I meant by "all this." The sweep of my hand took in the alchemist's nightmare ... and the people who operated it.

"They will be released," said Philip Wildeblood. His voice was calm, unruffled. Majestic, I suppose you might call it, if you wanted to. Like a king who has power and an absolute right to use it.

He wasn't ashamed. It just made no impression on him.

"And what happens to you when the people get to know?" I asked. It wasn't the sort of question that Nathan would have wanted me to ask. But I wasn't feeling very discreet.

But Philip was no fool, either. He thought fast on his feet. In fact, I think he'd been holding the car up his sleeve for a long time.

"The man responsible would have been brought to trial," he said, smoothly. "But that may not be possible, now. Mr. Parrick tells me that you can help undo the work that *he* has done ... can help to free the colony from its addiction to the drug." The stress on 'he" was careful, but firm.

There were no prizes for guessing who had been picked out to carry the can. I looked at the water, which was settling now. I couldn't see the blood in it. The light was all wrong. Somewhere, he'd float up to the surface. Somewhere in the watery underworld. And then he'd sink again, carrying with him all the guilt, all the blame, all the sins, the sins of the fathers. . . .

Leaving Philip stainless in the public eye. Not dishonored. He could pose as the savior of his people. Freeing them from the insidious ravages of the evil Zarnecki.

And we were going to help him.

I glanced at Cade, hoping that he might want to argue. But he was nursing his bruised back, and looking quite serene. There was even the ghost of a smile. The king's right hand man was gone, and he was heir apparent.

I felt sick.

"In your own house," I hissed, my voice catching because my teeth were gritting againt the cold. "You're going to pretend that he ran this operation on his own, beneath the cellars of your ancestral home?"

"I trusted him," said Philip. His voice had an air of injured innocence about it. He was already playing his part. I listened to the echo crackling faintly like spitting fat.

"I'll bet you did," I said. "And suppose it was me that landed on top of the startled whaley? Suppose I was dead and he was standing here? Who'd be your scapegoat then?"

But I didn't have to ask. Zarnecki had been the only candidate. If I were dead they'd just have hung one more crime on his neck. Then they'd have disposed of him. They wouldn't have had to look far for a volunteer executioner. And Nathan . . . Nathan would have stood by and watched. He'd have disapproved, of course. But needs must when the devil drives . . .

The devil was driving this one, all right.

Nathan was beside me now, offering a hand to help me. I was wet through and aching, but I refused the hand. I pointed past him, and lost control of my temper.

"Are you going to let him get away with this?" I yelled. "Are you going to help him get away scot free?" The echoes danced and jangled, louder and more clamorous than before.

"It's not our world, Alex," said Nathan softly. "We aren't the law here. He is. He can't kill us now, but only because he knows that he needs us. And it's not only him. They *all* need us, Alex. Every last one. Without our help, there's going to be hell to pay here within the year. And it won't be Philip who'll pay. It will be the farmers and the fishermen. This way is the only way we're going to be allowed to help them. We have to take it. It's our job."

"You're a bastard," I said.

He replied: "That doesn't matter."

I pointed again to the grey-clad, white-skinned specters, who were watching us with pale, bright, uncomprehending eyes—fascinated, but without any hint of understanding.

"Look at them, Nathan!" I whispered. "Doesn't that mean anything? How many people . . . how many years?"

"We have to help them, Alex," he said. "And this is the only way. The only way we can."

I stood, shivering and silent.

"Let's go," he said. "You need a little help yourself."

"Politics," I said, "is the art of the attainable."

"That's right."

"Kilner was right," I told him. "If this is what it costs ... if this is what it means, to colonize other worlds, to make the star-worlds ours, then we should stay at home, on Earth. We shouldn't pollute the whole galaxy."

"You don't mean that," he said. "And it won't even make you feel better to say so. It's not for us to take revenge, even if you take it upon yourself to judge, Philip is only one man. If we save him along with the rest of the people—well, that's one more man saved. His power is subject to erosion now. He'll lose it, by degrees. Whatever he's guilty of, history will bury it. It doesn't matter."

I wished that I could believe him.

Still refusing his help, I got back up to the door. Philip and the two servants stood aside to let me lead the way. Nathan and Cade followed.

They didn't lock the door or shoot home the bolt. It wasn't necessary. The people in the caves weren't prisoners any more. Not prisoners of *that* kind. Only prisoners of what they were and what, somehow, they'd have to be taught not to be. Now, they were only casualties. Casualties of a war that wouldn't start, because we were going to prevent it.

It was all, I thought, as I set my foot on the first rung of the ladder whose full extent was now illuminated, one hell of a mess.

19

It took me a long time to decipher James Wilde-blood's message in full, when I finally did get the chance. But knowing, by now, most or all of the answers didn't fully alleviate my curiosity. I wanted to follow the whole thing through to its bitter end.

There were no real surprises in the document. But there was little in it which gave any extra insight into the complex web of Wildeblood's motives. Even at the end, the man himself remained rather enigmatic, and I was left groping in my imagination for a true understanding of his purposes and intentions.

First of all, the message gave directions as to how to descend from the house into the caves. It wasn't detailed. With regard to pitfalls, all it said was "beware". The whole thing, apart from the eccentric spelling, was difficult to follow because of its chopped language and lack of punctuation. There was little about it that was explicit ... Wildeblood was expecting a certain amount of initiative on the part of anyone who tried to make use of it.

There were a few notes on the extraction and purification process to which the spawn had to be subjected. Here, again, you really needed to be something of a chemist already to work out what was said. They were the sort of incomplete, abbreviated notes a man in a lab might make, in order that he might recall his procedure later, relying on a certain basic knowledge and familiarity with what was being done to be able to fill in the gaps.

It really wouldn't have been much use to my nameless associate and his band of outlaws. They just wouldn't have been able to make sense of it at all.

Finally, there were a couple of notes tacked on. One said that the use of the drug in the colony would have to be restricted or stopped if and when exploitation began to threaten the ecological balance of the sea. The other said that this enforcement would have to be imposed from outside, because the ruling group would not voluntarily relinquish a source of power and the colonists themselves would not voluntarily relinquish their habit. Corollary to this statement was the parenthetical remark that ignorance would prevent understanding—apparently referring to the fact that the nth generation colonists would not be in a position to know why it was imperative that use of the drug must be modified or abandoned.

Last of all there was another sentence, also tacked on to the second note, but to my mind somewhat separate from it. It simply said: *Other sources must not be used.*

This, too, would not have been comprehensible to anyone in the colony who had managed to decipher the message. No reason was given. The recipient was obviously expected to work it out for himself.

I did.

When I had, I began to suspect that just possibly that last sentence was the only essential part of the communication. There was no possible way I could be sure, but the more I thought about it the more it seemed that perhaps it made sense in terms of James Wildeblood's probable priorities. He was, after all, a man of science.

He had obviously expected Earth to recontact the colony sooner. On what basis he had anticipated this, I'm not sure. The colonies were sent out on the understanding that they had to make it on their own, that no help could ever be guaranteed. But Wildeblood hadn't believed that. He had thought that contact of a kind to be maintained. He hadn't foreseen an eighty year moratorium on star flight.

James Wildeblood had obviously had doubts about the stuff of which colonists were made, and he knew as well as anyone the kinds of difficulty which would beset a small community trying to establish itself on an alien world. There was, I believe, more to his decision to take-over the colony and determine its fortunes single-handed than the simple lust for power. He really believed that what he was doing was insuring the maximum probability of its success and that this end justified his means—means which even he probably considered foul rather than fair.

Perhaps he expected a contact before he died. But when none came, he prepared a little legacy. A letter addressed to someone from Earth . . . to a scientist from Earth. The difficulty was making sure that it would be delivered, and it was an almost insurmountable one. Even to give it a chance he had to take certain unorthodox steps. He had to arrange things so that no one in the colony could read it, and that to find out what it said they would have to consult someone who could . . . someone from Earth. He had to make sure that it would stay in existence, and for this reason he manufactured rumors about its possible purpose—rumors about its connection with the liberation of the people from tyrannic rule. These methods were not certain to work, but they had a chance, and, as things had turned out, they had just about (but only just) done the trick.

What Wildeblood had not anticipated was the

fact that Earth had not the power to exercise any kind of authority over the colonies. We had not come armed with the power to compel the colonists to change their ways. But we were late, and we had arrived at a time when the means of persuasion were all set to come to hand, the exhaustion of the known supply.

One circumstance, and one alone, had permitted the story to reach the end that James Wildeblood had planned. That was the fact that his descendants had not found the alternative supply. They had not looked very hard. While the private and secret supply had been enough, they had stuck to it ... simply because it had all the advantages associated with privacy and secrecy. Only when it was threatened had Philip and Zarnecki finally been prepared to face the difficulties attendant upon opening up a new supply, and they had been too slow.

They had, perhaps, sent out ships to other islands, to look for another set-up similar to the one James Wildeblood had found. They had not been fortunate. The odds were far too long. But they had not looked beyond that possiblity. They had not thought of the *other* source—the *real* alternative.

The one that, to James Wildeblood's mind, *must* not be used.

The drug was extracted from the spawn of Poseidon's amphibians. The whaleys were most prolific in producing it, but they were not the only group of species which produced usable raw material. The smallest species, of course, did not produce enough for it to be worth exploiting them. But there were the intermediates ... including the salamen.

The salamen not only offered *a* potential alternative, but *the* potential alternative. The only way to find another whaley breeding ground was to search for one—its discovery would have to be a matter of luck. But the salamen were intelligent. They could communicate. They *knew* where their breeding grounds were.

And if that thought had occurred to a man like Zarnecki, or a man like Philip Wildeblood . . .

James Wildeblood had done his best to see that it would not occur to them. He had never tried to make contact with the salamen, had initiated a policy of let well alone which had been carried on by all the generations that came after. They saw no reason to be interested in the salamen. There was no one in the colony with anything like Conrad's priorities and interests.

James Wildeblood had had priorities somewhat akin to Conrad's. He had been willing to dominate and exploit his fellow men, but he had not been willing to see that exploitation extended to the alien indigenes . . . not, that is, if he could help it.

After realizing all that, I had a better, and maybe kindlier, picture of James Wildeblood's personality. I had a better idea of what made him tick. But the fact remained that all his ingenuity had been made necessary by his own actions. He tried to protect the salamen—but it had been he that exposed them to a terrible danger in the first place. All his desperate cunning had been directed toward the ultimate undoing of what he had, in the first place, done. *Why*, given his priorities, should he have put the salamen at risk in the first place?

You can answer that several ways. Maybe he wanted to give the colony every chance of success. Maybe he believed that if he hadn't done what he did the venture would have failed. Maybe he anticipated Kilner's findings—a host of colonies which had never surmounted their intitial difficulties, but had been forced to fight a long, long battle against circumstance which they were always losing, never able to turn the corner that would put them on the right road. Maybe he believed very deeply and very sincerely in the colony project, and thought that any gamble was justifiable if it would only insure success.

That's one way of looking at it. There's another.

Maybe his own intellectual values, his sense of right and wrong, his concept of the universe outside and beyond himself stood in contrast to and in conflict with a deep-seated urge to win personal power. Men have an almost limitless capacity for hypocrisy, for doublethink, for the simultaneous maintenance of contradictory systems of thought which govern action. Maybe he was impelled to both the doing and the undoing by simultaneous forces he would not choose between or control. Maybe he wanted to keep his cake and eat it too.

Take your choice. I've never taken mine, because I've never felt sure enough to pretend that I could. One way or another, Wildeblood did what he did. If we were to call up his ghost and ask him, he'd tell us that the reality was the former case. And he'd certainly believe it. But mightn't that be just one more rationalization built to bridge the hypocritical doublethink of the second case?

We'll never know. There's no way we can. Even Wildeblood could never really know. He could never be sure of himself. I think that showed in what the cryptogram said, and the way it said it.

But one way or another, it worked. The problem, so far as it could be, was "solved." I can't say that I, personally, was happy with the solution. It left Philip in power, the crimes of his forefathers conveniently banished and buried. It left the system pretty much the way it was. To me, it was a repair job where what was really called for was a total replacement, but my opinions didn't matter much in the scheme of things.

I did what I had to do.

The drug had to go. Completely. It wasn't enough to free the colonists from dependence in the physiological sense. The drug had to be outlawed, made unattractive and useless. (Quite apart from our reasons, there was political expediency. If Philip was losing a means of exercising power over the people he wasn't going to let that means be used by others. It had to be completely extinguished.)

What I did was to design a virus—a harmless thing that would become endemic in the colony, infecting every human body therein. Its sole function would be to act as a kind of extra chromosome, operating only one genetic faculty. It carried a blueprint for an enzymic antibody which would attack and break down a particular class of supersteroid molecules.

While the virus remained endemic—and it would sustain itself by normal processes of self-replication and infection—no one in the colony could ever get high on the drug again.

The drudge-work associated with the scheme consisted of helping the colony over its withdrawal symptoms. We controlled the release of the manufactured virus very carefully, limiting its rate of geographical spread. Because the colony was distributed over a whole chain of islands this wasn't difficult. Thus we could handle the problem in stages, with the aid of a couple of specially-trained local medical "flying squads."

It wasn't pleasant and it wasn't easy—for the colonists or for us. Getting people off an addiction bandwagon is always a touchy business. But we did it.

And while we did it, Philip's publicity machine

pronounced him a hero. He it was who was represented as freeing his people from a curse put upon them by evil conspirators led by Zarnecki. According to his propaganda the cyptogram became what rumor had always suggested that it was—a legacy from James Wildeblood to the colony, the means to free them from their curse. Unfortunately, the whole thing had been subverted by evil men.

I was sure that even if I'd been a village idiot I'd have been able to spot the load of lies for what it was. There were holes in the story you could drive a battleship through. But people have quite some capacity for believing what they're told, even when it doesn't make sense, provided that they're told loud enough and often enough. They swallowed it.

The leader of the revolution, whose name I never did discover, didn't end up in the mines. The new regime made him an offer he couldn't refuse, and he switched sides. What his erstwhile friends thought about it, I can only conjecture. I stopped thinking of him as Cyrano de Bergerac. Cyrano would *never* have sold out. Only people without the essentials of heroism do that.

And people like me, perhaps, if I'm not already included in that description.

For myself, I believed that I hadn't sold out *very much*. Sometimes it was easy to believe that, sometimes not. The people in the cave who had gathered the spawn and processed it and lived their lives entirely in darkness and by the feeble glow of electric lights were released. But they never could adapt fully to real life. I gave them what medical help I could, but it wasn't entirely a medical problem. That was when it wasn't so easy to believe. They would always be strangers, always fugitives, in their new world, and what kind of world is one "that hath such people in it"? Not brave, I think. Not brave at all.

But life, like or unlike politics, is the art of the attainable. It is what we can do, not what we ought to be able to do. The conditions in which we are permitted to exist are not ideal. Compromise, no matter how we may detest its individual cases, inevitably claims us, day by day, year by year. We have to do what we can within our limitations. And if we have done that, and succeeded, may we not believe that we are ahead of the game?

And, of course, there was more to it still. This is not the sum of what we did on Poseidon or its end. There remain another set of priorities, another set of ambitions. There was something accomplished there which needs not be tainted in the memory by guilt or shame or any other shadow of the conscience...

20

———◦◦◦———

"We're in the home stretch," said Conrad. "We have a vocabulary of a hundred and eighty signs. We're adding more every day. It's derived principally from their own language, of course, but we're modifying it somewhat. We'll be able to introduce new concepts and new constructions very soon. Mariel knows it all, of course, and it's all due to her that we're progressing so quickly. Linda is trying to keep up. The only one of us who can't attempt a decent conversation is me—and that's because I have to spend all my time collating the information, making a proper record and idly chatting to you."

"How many of them are involved?" I asked.

"Six or seven of them seem to have been allowed to work with us full time. How many in total know what's going on and have shown an interest I don't know. Maybe twenty or thirty. All ages, both sexes. Mariel reckons we'll be reaching the linguistic standard of first-season first-time terrestrial juvenile any day now. The parallel won't be exact, of course, but approximately. They don't use a vast number of words—maybe four hundred are in everyday use by the adults, and there isn't a great deal of esoteric extension to that. But by the time we start talking in earnest . . . who can tell how much expansion they can take?

"Linda is teaching three of them to draw the signs. She's working out a series of pictographs. The idea has caught on. We've given them writing.

189

We have no inkling yet of how much they'll want to say . . . how much they can *discover* to say.

"Mariel's been with them into the interior. They're showing her their territory, letting her see how they live. In her head, she's half gone native. She can imagine, somehow, the way they see the world, the natural avenues of their thought processes. She's becoming, in part of her mind, genuinely alien . . . and she can take it. She can control it. It isn't hurting her. She's right, Alex . . . this is the real *meaning* of her talent. This is what it's *for*.

"What we're doing here is big, Alex. It's interference on a scale we'd only imagined might be possible. We're altering the social evolution of this species. We're creating them, in a historical sense. Maybe that's not entirely right . . . we run the risk of making this particular group into aliens among their own kind. Maybe we have no moral right to interfere. But it's marvellous. It's the most important thing that has happened on any of the worlds we've visited. Here, we're proving something. We're proving that we can talk, we can meet, we can think and act together. Man and alien. Not even man and humanoid . . . man and amphibian.

"We've succeeded here, Alex. Over and beyond anything that the colony ever does or can do. We've achieved something that means a lot in a much greater context than human political affairs. We've opened up a new avenue in the whole scheme of universal existence . . .

"In the evenings, you know, when it's twilight, they go down into the shallows, to meet the others—the aquatics. I've watched them. Soon, I'm going with them; they'll introduce me. Isn't that something? A salamander introducing me to a tadpole . . . the effect that we're having on the terrestrials is being passed on. Back into the sea, into the cycle. Round and round . . . phase to phase, birth to birth. From now on, all the salamen, maybe, will be a little bit human. Earth has put a colony here, but maybe the significant colonization, in the long run, will be the colonization of ideas . . . that *means* something . . . on the *evolutionary* timescale."

"Sure," I said, trying to bring him down a little. "You like Playing God. So did God. And look where it got *us*."

He wasn't listening. He was immune from sarcasm, from clever words and cynical thoughts. He was thinking on another plane—*not* a divine plane, but a plane where there was a different kind of importance, a different order of magnitude in action and ambition.

He, too, had manufactured a virus that would infect a world. A virus of thought, of ways of thinking, of ideas. From now on, he had said, all salamen might become a little bit human . . .

Philip Wildeblood might rule another forty years. His sons and their sons—the whole dynastic sequence—might last a couple of hundred or a thousand. In historical terms, Philip's guilt or innocence, his whole effect on the pattern of life, would become meaningless in the blink of an eye. He'd been prevented from performing what might have proved to be the only meaningful and consequential action available to him—the initiation of a particularly nasty form of parasitism, human on native. Now that possibility was averted, he was nothing . . . or *almost* nothing. (There was still the margin, still the taint.)

But what Mariel and Conrad were doing might be meaningful a million years from now. It might change the very face of creation on this world we had named Poseidon. They could do in a year what the whole Poseidon colony had not done in a century.

And there was the converse, too. What was happening was an exchange, not a gift. Perhaps, if the salamen were to be a little bit human from now until forever, we, too, must become a little bit alien. Mariel already was, and always would be. Must that infection spread, like a manufactured virus, from mind to mind, from now on...?

Conrad thought that because of what was happening on Poseidon, man's place in the universe was no longer the same—that it had not merely changed, but changed in some definite and ultimately significant way.

And if he was right....

So much for the art of the attainable.